A Single Shot

A Single Shot

ROBBIE MACNIVEN

Sniper Elite: A Single Shot

First published 2026 by Rebellion
an imprint of Rebellion Publishing Ltd,
Riverside House, Osney Mead,
Oxford, OX2 0ES, UK

www.solarisbooks.com

ISBN: 978-1-83786-655-7

A CIP catalogue record for this book is available from the British Library.

Typeset by Andy Severn

Printed by Ingram Spark

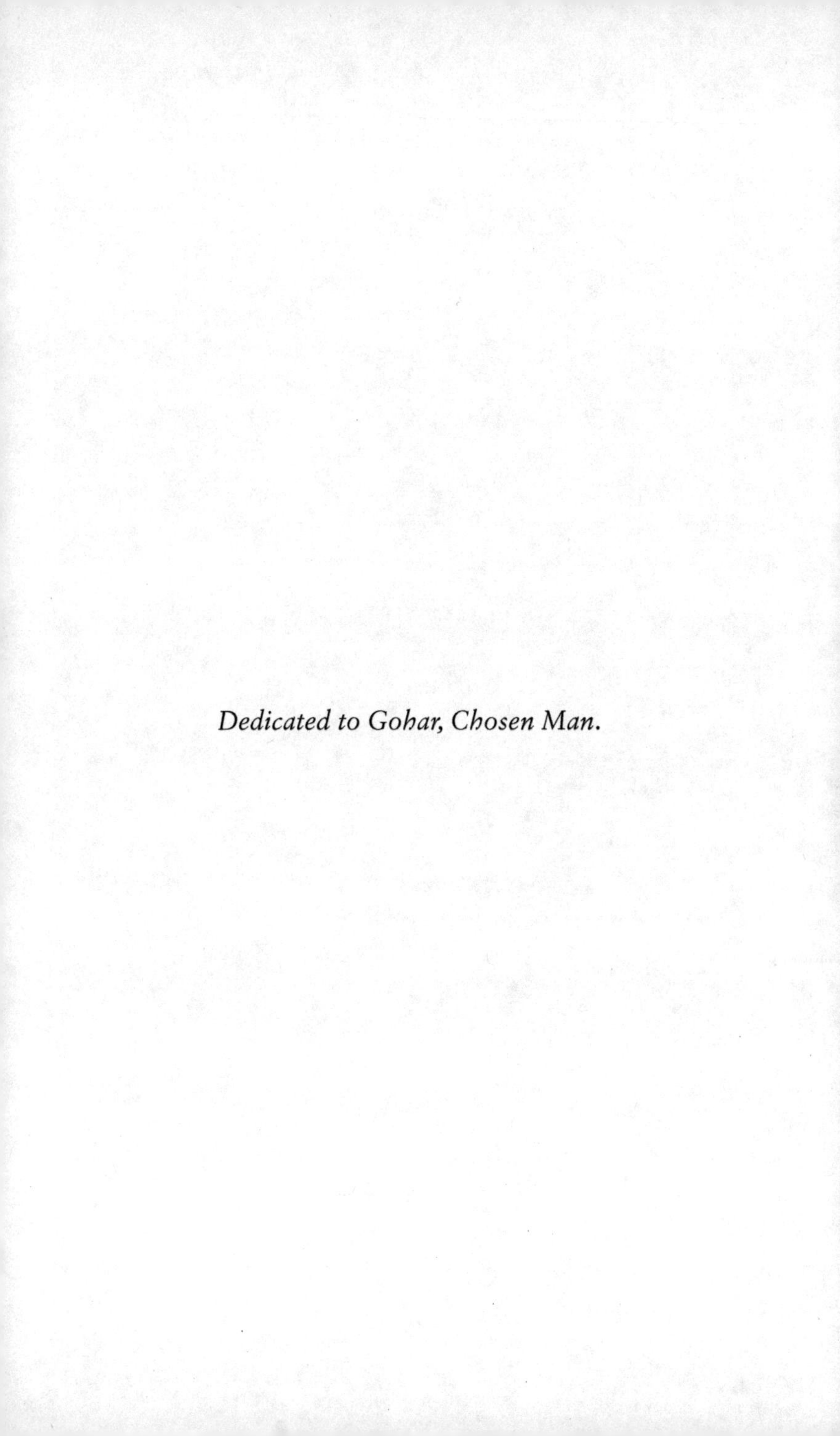

Dedicated to Gohar, Chosen Man.

But the Light Infantry Man, in particular, must not neglect his Arms, his Ammunition or throw away his Fire, as his Existence may depend upon a Single Shot's taking place.

– George Townshend, "Rules and Orders for the Discipline of the Light Infantry Companies in His Majesty's Army in Ireland," 1772.

Prologue

Cacabelos, Northern Spain,
January 3rd, 1809

The British were running, and dying, and Thomas Plunket had endured enough of it.

He ran too, but it wasn't away from the French cavalry who had spent that bitterly cold morning chasing down and sabring fleeing men. It was towards them, and towards the bridge they were about to cross, two arches of old Galician stone spanning the River Cua.

'Plunket, God damn it, come back!'

The words of his captain rang out after him, but he ignored them, leaving behind the three other men that formed his link in the skirmish chain – Mackintosh, Smith and Jones – and bounding down the slope towards the bridge. He darted left, right and left again so his worn leather shoes didn't slip in the snow and ice and mud. His heart was pounding, his hands freezing around the walnut stock of his Baker rifle. His thoughts burned with a grim, bloody-minded determination.

It had been three days since New Year and nine since, on Christmas Day, the bold British thrust into French-occupied Spain had turned into a retreat. The army had altered its course north-west, reaching the high country of Galicia, a place of steep slopes and narrow passes and winding tracks navigating plunging gorges and fast-flowing rivers, all held in midwinter's bitter grip. They were running for the coast and praying that the Royal Navy's ships would be there to provide a means of escape when they arrived. *If* they arrived.

Plunket reached the rutted roadway at the foot of the slope and stopped. The bridge lay ahead, with a small church, a mill and a copse of trees on its immediate left, and a series of walled gardens on its right, all struck bare and desolate by winter's withering touch. The bridge itself was perhaps four hundred yards away. Twice the recommended range for a Baker rifle, and too far for anyone in the regiment to hit a mark. Any rifleman, but Private Plunket.

There were bodies near where he had stopped in the road, frozen hard and half-covered with snow. The wreckage of an ammunition wagon stood off to one side, dismantled after it had thrown its axle. All along, the route both ahead and behind was littered with more detritus – abandoned canteens and shakos and muskets, belts and bayonets and cartridge pouches, knapsacks and haversacks, split and their contents spilt in the icy mud. The wreckage of defeat, of an army that was being marched to death.

And there was still so far to go. The old soldiers said it was hardship beyond any they had known, even in the campaigns in the Low Countries. Men froze to death, or starved to death, or dropped down dead from exhaustion, or shot themselves. There had been riots the night before, as starving, freezing soldiers fought each other for bread and shelter and got drunk on plundered wine. Just up the road the commander of the rearguard, General Paget, had spent the morning hanging the worst offenders.

Plunket dared advance a little further down the road before assessing the distance again, checking the wind. Then, he did something that must have seemed strange and ridiculous to the French cavalry about to enter the bridge. He took off his shako and lay down on his back.

Briefly, his world was reduced to the cold, hard earth under him and the low slate-grey clouds above. He shifted, settling himself, looking down the length of his body towards the bridge, and the enemy. Ordinarily, his knapsack, strapped to his back, would have made the position more cumbersome, but the colonel had ordered the 95th to abandon either their greatcoats or their packs by the road a few days earlier, to further speed the retreat, and Plunket didn't know of a single man who had elected to keep his knapsack instead of his coat.

He moved slightly to his right, the flat, frozen ground of the roadway a preferable position to the snowy tussocks on either side. Along it he could see French light cavalry preparing to cross the bridge, hussars in fine green and gold uniforms and tall, furred hats. Swift, arrogant and ruthless, the terror of every light infantryman. They had fallen on the raggedy British rearguard earlier that morning as they had tried to hold the village on the far side of the river, a little hamlet of rough stone houses and timber outbuildings called Cacabelos. Panic had gripped the British, and there had been a desperate rush for the bridge as the enemy horsemen had sabred and slashed their way through the rearmost ranks. Plunket had seen dozens of men from his own regiment, the 95th Rifles, hacked down, warm blood steaming in the frigid air. Even the commanding general himself, Sir John Moore, had become caught up in the chaos and had almost been captured.

But the eagerness of the French vanguard to hunt the hated, green-jacketed riflemen through the narrow streets had worked against them. They had become scattered around the village, and the main body of the British rearguard – including the general – had made it over the Cua. Now they were hastening to form on the bank opposite Cacabelos, the redcoats of the 28th Regiment of Foot blocking the roadway behind Plunket, the 52nd Regiment to his right, while the 28th's light company and the Rifles formed a skirmish chain ahead of them. Behind, further up the slope, was a battery of guns from the Royal Horse Artillery, hastily unlimbering and swabbing out their barrels just below the crest.

The British were nearly ready to receive the enemy on their own terms, but the French had reformed as well, and the hussar squadrons, packed into a column four horsemen wide and stretching back into Cacabelos, were about to cross the bridge. If they weren't slowed, the retreat would become a rout, and if the rearguard broke again, it would all be over. The French would fall upon the remnants further along the road, and Britain's only field army would be destroyed.

Plunket had broken formation and dashed forward on a sudden, determined impulse. About three hundred yards now, he thought, still assessing the range while lying on his back. He brought his left leg over his right, as a man reclining on a padded chair might while engaged in conversation, then laid his rifle along the length of his body, the brass-bound butt secured against his right armpit, the barrel resting on the crook of his foot and its black leather sling looped around his shoe and tugged tight and firm against the sole.

He could see the leading hussars, just about to reach the bridge. A man rode ahead of them, crossing before the main body of cavalry. He wore a jacket of blue and gold, straight-backed in his saddle, riding atop a white horse. A senior officer, cantering ahead to reconnoitre the ground and ensure it was fit for his squadrons.

A rich man, Plunket thought, with a fine uniform and a fine steed. A brave man, leading his cavalry from the front, the very tip of the spear. A foolish man, believing himself still far outside the range of British muskets, not noticing – or perhaps simply disdaining – the green-clad rifleman on the roadway ahead of him.

A dead man, if Plunket had anything to do with it.

He eased his rifle's flint back to full cock, hearing that dull, satisfying click. Then, he settled the front and rear sights on the officer, drawing a line just above the man's large bicorn hat.

A few heartbeats, and then he eased the breath out of his lungs, not expelling it forcefully, simply pausing ahead of his next inhalation.

Both eyes open, the way his father had taught him, while they had stalked game across the fields and forests of Wexford County.

Softly, he squeezed the trigger.

The priming powder in the pan ignited with a flash, sending flame searing through the touchhole and setting off the main charge in the breech. The rifle butt kicked against his armpit and shoulder, and the muzzle spat fire and smoke past his leg, the percussive bang beating at his ears.

He moved immediately, rolling to the side so he could see past the smoke of his own shot, the motion made clumsy and cumbersome by his greatcoat and freezing limbs.

There was a moment's savage exultation as he saw that the shot had struck true. The officer had lurched forward over his horse's neck, and as Plunket watched, he toppled sideways from the saddle with a strange, slow grace.

The cavalry behind, still yet to fully cross the bridge, pulled up short at the sight of their commander's collapse, but one man rode on. He was another officer, some sort of aide or subaltern. He reached the spot where his superior had fallen on the near bank and began to dismount.

Plunket already knew what the likes of Mackintosh, Smith and the other third-class shots of the regiment would say when he made it back to the company. A one-off. A lucky shot.

Lucky shot be damned, Plunket thought, as he stayed on his side and brought the muzzle down alongside his body. He pulled the flint back until it clicked once, at half cock, and primed the barrel from his powder flask, then reached into one of the black leather pouches on the belt worn over his greatcoat to retrieve a small patch of cloth, cut from old bedding and greased on both sides. He centred it over the muzzle and held it in place with one finger while, with his other hand, he retrieved a musket ball from a second pouch.

It wasn't easy reloading prone, but the Baker rifle's barrel – almost nine inches shorter than the smoothbore India pattern Brown Bess muskets used by the regular infantry – made it more feasible. Calloused, frigid hands didn't help either, but Plunket was moving through the motions automatically now, the reloading an activity he had long ago relegated to muscle memory, even if he could barely feel the tips of his fingers.

He pressed the ball into the patch centred over the muzzle and down as far as he could into the barrel, then slid the steel ramrod out and, without reversing it, forced the ball and patch the rest of the way. He gritted his teeth as he rammed it to the base of the bore, the patch making it more difficult compared to a paper cartridge.

The patch was the key though, along with the spiralling grooves within the barrel's bore, the rifling. Those grooves would cause any fired projectile to start to spin mid-flight, lending it greater accuracy than one that did not. Yet a musket ball could not be trusted to fit snugly enough to catch the grooves as it was blasted free, so the patch wrapped around it did the gripping instead, rotating rapidly as it left the barrel and causing the bullet held in it to spin as it flew.

Plunket snatched a glance up as he worked. The French aide had dismounted and now had his arms under his superior's, half lifting him, half dragging him back towards the bridge, where the rest of the cavalry had stalled.

A few more thrusts ensured both patch and musket ball were properly sited. He then returned the rammer and primed the pan with more gunpowder. Normally, priming was the first loading step, but riflemen often performed it last when loading with patch and ball, to ensure the air expelled through the touchhole by ramming the main charge down the barrel didn't blow the fine grains of black powder out of the open pan.

He snapped the hammer shut, then dropped onto his back again, regaining the supine position.

Butt into pit of the arm, cock eased back for the second click, the spring mechanism fully engaged. Barrel resting against the crossed leg, its strap pulled taut around his foot.

He lined the front and back sights up, adjusted fractionally.

The world seemed to become as still and frozen as the ice scumming the top of the River Cua. Plunket squeezed the trigger.

Another discharge, but this time instead of rolling he scrambled to his feet, forcing tired, stiff limbs to obey.

The cheering from the greenjackets back up the slope told him the outcome before he saw it for himself through the smoke. The second officer had fallen, slumped motionless atop the first. His horse had bolted, clattering back over the bridge.

Plunket found himself grinning. He stooped to snatch up his shako, just as the sound of a cavalry trumpet pealed out over the river.

Seemingly without further orders, the French cavalry charged, pounding across the bridge and over the bodies of their fallen leaders. Suddenly, the hard earth was shivering with the hammering of hundreds of hooves.

Plunket turned and raced back up the slope. There was a crash like thunder, loud enough for him to feel it punch against his chest – several of the Royal Artillery guns that had unlimbered just below the crest had fired over the heads of the infantry further down the slope. He heard the rumble of round shot passing above but didn't look round to witness the solid balls ploughing red furrows through the oncoming enemy.

His section of the skirmish chain reached for him and pulled him into their midst, still cheering and grinning. Hands clapped his shoulders and back and gripped his arm as he looked along the line and saw a gaggle of British officers cantering on horseback along the slope. He recognised the red-coated officer in the lead as General Paget, commander of the rearguard.

The horsemen slewed to a stop along the back of the skirmish chain, hooves slipping in the icy muck, and Plunket brought his rifle to the salute as a sudden silence fell around him.

'You made those shots?' Paget demanded, looking down on him.

'That I did, sir,' Plunket replied, keeping his expression neutral now, refusing to allow his pride to show to a senior officer.

'What's your name?'

'Corporal Plunket, sir. Thomas Plunket.'

'Well, that was the damned coolest piece of shooting I've ever seen, Corporal Plunket, and to do it twice… couldn't be less than three hundred yards, maybe more.'

'Just thought I should give them one or two back, sir.'

'Quite so, man, quite so. You know about the bounty?'

'What bounty, sir?' Plunket asked, keeping a straight face, though several of the riflemen around him found their voices and began to jeer good-naturedly.

'A reward for every French officer bagged,' Paget said. 'Here—'

The general fished into his sabretache and pulled out a small leather purse. Plunket caught it, hearing it clink and feeling the weight of it in his hand.

'Follow this man's example, and we'll see old England again soon enough,' Paget called out to the rest of the riflemen, as cheering began to spread along the extended line. 'I'd much rather be rewarding fine marksmanship than hanging mutinous dogs for looting and rioting! You do the army proud, Plunket. Keep it up.'

Plunket called out his thanks, but Paget and his subalterns were already spurring off along the line. He finally allowed himself to grin once more.

The French cavalry came on over the bridge, but now the British weren't running. The skirmish line began to fire, and seconds later the 52nd, moving up from the flank, added a battalion volley, the noise clapping back from the high hills surrounding Cacabelos, smoke and lead crashing over the Cua. The front ranks of the cavalry were tumbled in bloody ruin, men and horses screaming. The artillery on the upper slope thundered again, switching to canister now, a blizzard of lead balls whipping the oncoming column raw and blasting powdered stone from the bridge's flank.

Channelled by the narrowness of the crossing, the hussars had nowhere to go but on, into the maelstrom. By some desperate miracle, a few survived, horses vaulting the thrashing, wounded beasts in front of them, steel hooves striking sparks from bloody cobbles. The riders threw themselves on and up the slope towards the closest redcoats, the light company of the 28th. Steel flashed and sabres clashed against lunging bayonets, but the horsemen were now far too few to threaten even a single company. Soon they were all dead or taken, their remaining comrades retreating back into the narrow streets and lanes of Cacabelos.

The rearguard would not collapse, not today. Thanks to two good shots, the retreat would continue.

Chapter One

Outside Badajoz, Spain,
October 5th, 1809

'IT'S A DAMNED problem, is what it is,' the Duke of Wellington growled.

'Problems exist to be solved,' Mister Simpson responded obsequiously.

Wellington resisted the urge to snap at the horrid man, settling instead for glaring at him from across the table.

The other officers present in the room said nothing. The commandeered farmhouse they were occupying was the headquarters of the army's Third Division, but Wellington had ousted their staff that morning at Simpson's request. He had ridden east from his own headquarters in the walled town of Badajoz specifically for this meeting. Wellington considered the disruption a necessary evil, much like Simpson himself.

'The important thing is that we now know the source of the enemy's recent superiority,' the man was saying, apparently unperturbed by Wellington's cold, level gaze. 'Which means we can now act decisively against it, Your Grace.'

'I suppose,' Wellington growled, leaning back in his chair and turning his eyes down, to the maps spread across the table before him.

"*Your Grace.*" The title was one he was still getting used to. News of its conference had reached Portugal a little over a month ago – by appointment of His Majesty, he was now no longer Sir Arthur Wellesley, but Viscount

Wellington of Talavera and Baron Douro of Wellesley. A reward for defeating Marshal Soult's army earlier that year, a few days march north-east of where the British were now encamped.

Right now, both the honours and the victory itself felt hollow. Wellington might have won the day at Talavera, but it had been earned with blood, and the campaign had ended with a hasty retreat, as multiple French columns had closed in and threatened to cut his little army's line of communications back to Portugal. Since then, he had adopted a defensive posture and put his divisions into winter quarters along the banks of the Guadiana River, hoping against hope that further French reinforcements in the spring would be delayed, and that the vast stocks of arms and ammunition at the enemy's disposal might be depleted by rain and raids conducted by Spanish partisans.

At least now Wellington understood just where the enemy's seemingly inexhaustible munitions were coming from, at a time when it felt as though every single cartridge and cannonball owned by the British forces in the Peninsular was precious. Simpson's report had identified the problem. Now, as Simpson had said, all they had to do was fix it.

'You're sure it's this place at Zaragoza?' Wellington asked, looking back up at his spymaster. Simpson was a rotund and ruddy-faced fellow, with a mouth that seemed constantly on the cusp of a tight, sly smile, twinned with eyes that looked like they never smiled at all. He was technically a major in the British Army but always wore drab civilian garb. Wellington was not aware of his true identity, or even any name or alternative title besides that of "Mister Simpson." Whitehall had sent him and, despite Wellington's ongoing misgivings, he had proven his value.

'We are sure, Your Grace,' said Simpson to Wellington. He always referred to himself with a plural pronoun, an affectation that annoyed Wellington, but which he supposed was designed to hint at the great many peoples caught up in Mister Simpson's webs, at the many personalities that fuelled the knowledge that made him so indispensable to Britain's war against Bonaparte in Spain.

'Several separate partisan groups have reported it, including one from within the factory itself,' he went on.

'And you trust them?' Wellington demanded. The Spanish guerrillas had made the previous year of occupation hellish for the French, but they were a raggedy bunch with no centralised command, and their effectiveness varied from one group to the next. Some were little better than opportunistic bandits, others even supplied intelligence to the French in exchange for gold and supplies.

'This particular band I trust, yes,' Simpson said. 'Their leader, El Cruz, was an officer in the regular army before the collapse last summer. He's captured over a dozen French couriers in the vicinity of Zaragoza since then, but he doesn't have the numbers to properly threaten their supply lines.'

Wellington refrained from commenting on the effectiveness – or ineffectiveness – of the regular Spanish Army, and what that meant about the likes of El Cruz.

'Regardless, I will not authorise an expedition to Zaragoza,' he told Simpson firmly. 'I'm stretched thin enough as it is. If Marshal Soult renews his offensive, it'll be the devil to pay.'

'Of course,' Simpson said. 'But El Cruz does not believe they can do anything to curtail production on his own. That is why I requested the presence of Lieutenant Colonel Robertson. As you know, he has been of some... assistance to us in matters like this in the past.'

Wellington glanced towards the three other officers in

the room, all stood to one side. Two were mere youths, Lieutenants Fraser and Aird, red-coated subalterns from Wellington's staff. The other was older, more senior, and wore not scarlet, but the dark green and black-faced jacket of the 95th Rifles. His name was Lieutenant Colonel Robertson, and it was Mister Simpson who had requested his presence at the meeting.

'What do you make of all of this, Robertson?' Wellington demanded of him. 'Sounds like it could be a deadly little business. I would understand if you don't want any of your men seconded to such an… escapade.'

'On the contrary, sir,' Robertson said with a ghost of a smile. 'I already have just the man in mind.'

'Is that so?' Wellington said. 'Is he bivouacked nearby?'

'He should be with the pickets just north of the Guadiana, sir. Though that's no guarantee. He has a habit of abandoning his post.'

'Abandoning his post? Hardly sounds like the sort of fellow we need for a job like this.'

'Well, when he does abandon it, sir, it's usually to go hunt the enemy.'

Wellington raised an eyebrow, then snapped at one of the subalterns.

'Mister Fraser! Make yourself useful man and take a ride to the pickets. You're to retrieve – what was his name, Robertson?'

'Corporal Plunket, sir. Thomas Plunket.'

'The Cacabelos marksman?' Wellington asked, betraying a moment's surprise.

'Some call him that, sir, yes.'

Wellington pondered the identity, then carried on giving Fraser his instructions.

'Go and find Corporal Plunket of the 95th and get him back here. Tell him we've got a task for him. Tell him one shot could make or break this entire war.'

Chapter Two

North of the Guadiana, Spain,
October 5th, 1809

LIEUTENANT WILLIAM FRASER rode through the lines of the Third Division's bivouacs and crossed over the Guadiana, then took a goat track north to where the pickets were guarding the furthest edges of Wellington's encamped army. He paused to speak to a detachment of the 45th Foot, who pointed him east along a low ridge to where the 95th's outposts were. There, he met a Rifles captain who said he had given permission to Corporal Plunket and a few other men to advance out beyond the lines to investigate reports from Spanish villagers that there were French foragers in the area.

Fraser rode on, privately thrilled to be straying so far from headquarters. It had been impossible to turn down the honour of being assigned to the duke's staff, especially given the lengths his father, the reverend, had gone to in order to secure the position. Yet in the few months he had been serving in Spain he had found himself yearning for a more active role, to swap the endless courier duties for the adventure he had dreamt about when he had purchased his commission in the army. He hadn't even set eyes on a French soldier yet, much less seen any serious action.

His father would disapprove of that attitude, he knew. He should be happy with his lot and pleased with the fact he was doing his duty, regardless of how. At times, he even doubted what his own reaction might be when he eventually experienced the heat of combat. Such violence went so against his nature, against his upbringing, he felt sure he would freeze up, would be struck dumb with horror or indecision. Yet such unknowns only added to the allure of the whole thing.

As he rode on, he indulged himself by likening what he was doing to the efforts of Wellington's intelligence officers, those men who rode out fully uniformed – so they could not be hanged as spies if captured – and ranged the Spanish countryside collecting information on the enemy's dispositions and movements. It was their work, along with a constant stream of reports and rumours from the partisan bands, that fed the likes of Mister Simpson. Now, Fraser could imagine himself involved in that shadowy business, intent on striking a blow against the machinations of Old Boney.

He experienced a brief surge of panic when he almost rode into a pair of blue-jacketed horsemen in a vineyard beyond the ridgeline, before realising they were British videttes, light dragoons. They said they didn't know anything about riflemen ranging past the lines or word from the local peasantry, and cautioned Fraser that if he went any further, there were no guarantees he wouldn't fall foul of a French patrol. Officially, the nearest enemy concentration was far to the north, but their foraging parties were forever ranging south, close to British lines, working endlessly to feed the tens of thousands of French troops that Napoleon insisted live off the land they were occupying.

Fraser thanked the dragoons for their concern, then rode on. He passed an abandoned farmhouse and decided to leave the track and take to the next ridge, hoping he'd be able to see more of the surrounding countryside. He had just set his mount, Bucephalus, onto the slope when he heard the crack of a gunshot.

He looked left and right but could see no sign of where the sharp sound had come from. He touched his spurs to his mount's flanks and made hard for the ridge's crest, but just before he could reach it a figure burst from the cover of a straggly thicket of undergrowth and lunged at him.

Bucephalus shied and Fraser cried out, sawing on the reins and narrowly keeping his balance in the saddle, having to lean back hard. The man snatched at the horse's bridle, and Fraser was fumbling for his sword when he realised his assailant was in the raggedy dark green uniform of a British rifleman.

'Easy lad, easy,' the man said in a broad accent – a fellow Scot. 'Just didn't want you racing over the hill there and alerting the enemy.'

'The enemy?' Fraser asked, petting Bucephalus's neck in an effort to calm him while he tried to grasp the situation. 'I heard a gunshot—'

'Aye, you did, sir, as did we all. There's a bit of trouble brewing ahead. Best dismount. A man on a horse will stand out something fierce upon yonder crest, even before we consider that lovely scarlet coat of yours.'

Fraser hesitated, then did as advised, dismounting from Bucephalus and leading the stallion by the reins.

'The French are here?' he asked the rifleman, trying not to sound too excited.

'A patrol of froggy dragoons, out foraging,' the man responded. 'They've not spotted us yet, and we'd like to keep it that way for the time being.'

'Are you Plunket?' Fraser asked, the reason for his expedition reimposing itself at the forefront of his thoughts. 'Corporal Plunket? The duke has sent me to find him.'

The rifleman laughed as they neared the crest.

'No, I'm not Plunket. Mackintosh is the name. The corporal's just ahead though. What sort of trouble has he got himself into with the duke?'

Fraser checked himself before he revealed any details of the conversation at headquarters.

'All I know is that His Grace wishes to see him, and the matter is urgent,' he said instead. Mackintosh scoffed, then stopped Fraser again just below the crest.

'Best tie the horse, sir, and stick with me. I'm going to have to ask you to get low. That lovely coat may end up a little dirty.'

Fraser made no complaint, tying Bucephalus's reins to a stunted tree nearby before telling Mackintosh to lead on. His heart was racing, his throat dry. This was exactly the sort of escapade he'd hoped to find once he got out of headquarters.

They reached the crest, where Mackintosh dropped onto his hands and knees, his rifle slung across his back. Fraser did likewise, taking off his bicorn hat and hitching up his sword as best as he could, crawling awkwardly after the rifleman. They entered a dense patch of brittle, straggling undergrowth, and for a while he could see nothing of the rest of the slope and what lay beyond.

He crawled through the dirt and the dust, thorns snagging his arms and shoulders, then realised that Mackintosh had risen into a low stoop ahead, following a line of boulders that ran under the reverse side of the crest. Fraser kept with him, until Mackintosh came to a stop.

They had found another rifleman. He was lying on his front, knapsack off and propped against one boulder to his left, Baker rifle leaning against another on his right. He had a small telescope out and was looking through it between a break in the rocks, the brass tube resting against the stone.

There was another figure beside him, crouched in the cover of the rocks: a bedraggled Spanish boy with bare feet who stared, wide-eyed and silent, up at Fraser through a dense nest of dark hair.

'What is it?' the rifleman asked without taking his eye from the telescope.

'My name is Lieutenant William Fraser, I've just come from headquarters,' Fraser began to say, trying not to blurt the words out all at once. 'Are you Corporal Plunket?'

'Yes,' Plunket said.

'The general wishes to speak with you. I'm to take you back to divisional headquarters immediately.'

'Later,' Plunket murmured.

'Later?' Fraser repeated, surprised.

'That's what I said,' Plunket responded, finally turning away from his telescope and looking up at him. Fraser was taken aback by how young he looked – in his early twenties, he thought, not so much older than Fraser himself, with sharp, handsome features and pale blue eyes that gazed at Fraser with a kind of hawkish keenness.

'There are French dragoons at the far side beneath the ridge,' Plunket told him matter-of-factly. 'This boy here came running into our picket line an hour ago. I volunteered with a few of the lads to go and see what he was yammering about.'

'What're the French doing at the farm?' Fraser asked, knowing he shouldn't become distracted from his mission, but unable to help himself.

'See for yourself,' Plunket said, and shifted up into a crouch, vacating the space between the rocks. He handed Fraser the telescope and, after a brief hesitation, the lieutenant took it.

Fraser knelt awkwardly in the spot Plunket had been lying in and hunched forward until he was able to peer through the gap in the rocks. It took him a few seconds to align the telescope and understand what he was looking at.

Then, for the first time, he saw the French.

There was a farmhouse at the foot of the ridge, its walls cracked, whitewashed stone, appended by a barn and a few animal pens. A French dragoon, dressed in a green jacket and with a tall brass helmet crested with black horsehair, was leaving one of the pens with the limp body of a goat hefted over his shoulder. That had likely been the source of the gunshot Fraser had heard.

Two other dragoons, armed with carbines, were standing over several men, women and children, who had been made to kneel in the dust of the yard in front of the main building. Fraser assumed they were the family who owned the farm. He looked away briefly from the telescope at the boy hiding in the rocks beside them.

'*¿Ese es tu familia?*' he asked him. The boy blinked, seemingly surprised that he could understand what the red-coated stranger was saying. Then he nodded.

'You speak the lingo, do you?' Plunket muttered. Fraser looked back at him and nodded.

'Yes, my father made sure my education included—'

'Ask him how many horsemen came to the farm today,' Plunket interrupted. Fraser frowned, then addressed the boy again.

'*¿Cuántos jinetes viste?*'

'*Seis,*' the boy said solemnly.

'Six,' Fraser relayed to Plunket. The rifleman grunted.

'That's what I feared. There are only five Frenchies down there.'

'I only see three,' Fraser said, returning his eye to the telescope.

'Count the horses,' Plunket advised.

Fraser did so and discovered there were five horses tied to the fence posts outside the front yard.

'The other two are probably searching inside the farmhouse,' Plunket said. 'They wouldn't stray far from their mounts. But where's the sixth?'

The rifleman was silent before continuing.

'If I were in charge of those dragoons, I would put a horseman up on this ridge, as a lookout.'

Fraser instinctively looked to either side, half expecting to discover a French cavalryman suddenly bearing down on them, but their low position combined with the scrubland covering the slope meant he could see little of the rest of the ridge.

'He's probably on the crest, either further east or west of us,' Plunket said. 'You're lucky he didn't see your approach. I had Mackintosh out hunting for him when he ran into you instead.'

'I have orders to take you back to headquarters, immediately,' Fraser said, trying again to impress on Plunket the reason he had tracked him down.

'Tell the boy that,' Plunket said. Fraser felt brief confusion, before the rifleman went on. 'Tell that boy we're going to walk away while his family are robbed and murdered, because the duke wants a little chat.'

Fraser said nothing but instead looked back down at the farmstead.

Sure enough, two more dragoons were emerging from the main building, hefting full forage bags. The one with the slain goat had moved over to the horses and was securing the animal's corpse across the back of his mount.

'I think they're about to leave,' Fraser said.

'Then we're out of time,' Plunket said. 'Move aside.'

Fraser obeyed, and Plunket reclaimed his spot, except this time instead of resting his telescope between the rocks, he slid his rifle forward.

'Jones still in place?' he called out softly to Mackintosh, who had manoeuvred to the edge of the rocky outcrop, further off to the right. The other greenjacket signalled an affirmative, as Fraser craned up as much as he dared, realising there was at least one more rifleman concealed in the scrub nearby.

'Tell the boy to stay down,' Plunket told him as he settled the rifle. 'And when this starts, you're both to do exactly what I say, when I say.'

Fraser passed on the instructions in Spanish. It might have seemed outrageous for a lieutenant to be taking orders from a mere corporal, but it hadn't even occurred to him to attempt to take charge of the situation. He was suddenly and horribly aware of just how out of his depths he was.

Keeping his hat off, he edged a look over the top of the rocks.

At the same time, Plunket fired.

Chapter Three

North of the Guadiana, Spain,
October 5th, 1809

FRASER WATCHED THE two dragoons standing over the captured Spanish family, expecting one to reel back, struck dead by a pinpoint shot. Instead, it was the dragoon who'd been carrying the goat that reacted. The horse he was tying his prize to bolted, ripping itself free from the hitching post where it had been tied, while the other mounts reared and shrieked, the sound of their distress carrying up the ridgeline.

The two dragoons standing over the family turned about, looking for the source of the shot, before one identified the smoke from Plunket's discharge. He immediately fired his carbine up towards the rocks, but he was far out of range, and Fraser had no idea where the shot fell.

Plunket had started to reload, while Mackintosh broke right, racing towards a straggly tree a little further down the slope. The two dragoons who had emerged from the farmhouse had discarded their loot and were running towards their horses.

Fraser looked back to Plunket, who had finished priming his rifle. The Spanish family had flung themselves behind the farmyard wall, seemingly forgotten now by their captors. The two dragoons who had been carrying the loot successfully mounted their horses, while the one who had shot the goat took one of his comrades' steeds. The trio began to spur towards the slope, while the other two ran forward behind them, clearly realising their carbines were out of range. They probably thought they were simply dealing with a few partisans taking pot-shots.

They were about to discover their mistake. The range from the farm to the ridge had been extreme, even for rifles, but the French were now closing that gap of their own accord, focused on Mackintosh, who they thought had been the source of the shot. Fraser watched the rifleman with some concern as he paused at the bare tree he had taken up position behind and took aim with the assistance of one of the lower branches. There was another gunshot, echoing flat over the ridgeline, and one of the horses went down in a flurry of dirt and kicking hooves, the rider landing badly.

The other two riders raked back their spurs, sensing the lone marksman was theirs for the taking – they would be on him before he could reload, and when a cavalryman caught an infantryman alone and with his gun empty, there was almost always only one outcome.

But of course, Mackintosh wasn't alone.

Plunket fired his second shot, and one of the dragoons was snatched from the saddle, his horse racing on. The third checked his charge, realising there was more than one shooter among the rocks. The two on foot who had been following up in support paused too, and one fired. This time, the shot was closer – Fraser heard it crack into stone somewhere nearby.

He realised the Spanish boy who had been next to Plunket was trying to scramble up onto the rocks to get a view of what was happening. He tugged him back into cover.

'Stay down,' he urged him in Spanish.

Likely understanding that hesitating now would be fatal, the last mounted dragoon rode hard at Mackintosh. Fraser clutched the hilt of his sword, feeling useless, helpless, only able to watch as the horseman closed the last few yards. Mackintosh was still ramming his second shot.

There was a puff of smoke from a patch of thorns further east, and abruptly the last rider fell, so close to Mackintosh the dragoon's horse had to swerve at the last moment to avoid the tree he had been sheltering behind. The sound of the shot reached Fraser – the third rifleman Plunket had mentioned earlier, Jones.

The two dragoons on foot began to retreat, back towards the farmyard and the one horse that was still hitched there. The dragoon unhorsed by Mackintosh during the charge clambered back to his feet, clutching an injured arm and beginning to scramble down the slope after his fleeing comrades.

The Spanish boy thrust past Fraser and began to run towards the farm.

'Oh, bless me,' Fraser gasped, the closest thing to a swear he regularly uttered, before shouting at the boy to stay back.

The youth either didn't hear or didn't care. Without thinking, Fraser set off after him.

He should have kept a grip on him, but now he was stumbling down the ridge, sword hitched and banging against his leg, feeling suddenly exposed as he left the rocks behind. One of the dismounted dragoons had turned back to face them and was trying to reload his carbine, but there was another shot from one of the riflemen. It was a miss, but close enough that it convinced the man to keep running.

'Stop,' Fraser panted breathlessly, stumbling on stones and straggling undergrowth, feeling a sense of despair as the gap between him and the boy extended. Several of the Spanish family had risen from behind the yard wall and were yelling at the child to go back.

Then, Fraser heard the hooves. He looked about wildly as he ran, and caught sight of another Frenchman, mounted, surging towards them both from the left. The sixth dragoon, the one Plunket had suspected was riding along the ridge nearby. The rifleman had been correct.

Fraser staggered to a halt and dragged his sword free of its scabbard. He found himself rooted, not knowing if he should keep going after the boy, or try to get back up the slope, or look for a tree or rock to put between himself and the dragoon. The man was leaning low in the saddle, brass helm gleaming, its black horsehair crest streaming. His sword caught the sunlight with a flash as he levelled it at Fraser.

He could hear someone shouting over the rising drumbeat of the hooves but didn't know who. He understood that he should raise his sword, but when he did the motion felt heavy and clumsy, as though he was trying to force someone else's arm up, rather than his own. His one remaining thought, as the thunder engulfed him, was relief at the realisation that the dragoon had chosen to ride him down, and not the boy.

There was a cracking sound, and the rider swerved. Fraser saw bright red blood, and then finally his instincts kicked in and he flung himself aside, almost crushed and trampled as the horse slammed past him.

He kept his footing and found himself looking down at a body – the dragoon's, tumbled from his mount. There was a hole in his left breast, staining the red facings of his green coat almost black.

The man was young, Fraser thought. His eyes stared up sightless at him, until the redcoat lieutenant turned away.

The remaining three dragoons were still fleeing, one managing to mount the last horse that was still hitched by the yard. He rode off, leaving the other two to escape on foot. The boy had made it to his family, scrambling over the farmyard wall. Fraser felt his strength suddenly leave him as he realised they were safe, and he had to make a conscious effort not to simply sit down in the dust.

He looked to the ridge, for the telltale skeins of smoke that would mark where one of the three riflemen had fired from. He could find none though, until he turned back towards the farmhouse. There, the dissipating smoke revealed a fourth greenjacket, perched on the low, tiled roof. It looked as though he had climbed up using a wooden outhouse leaning against the main building's flank.

The rest of the rifle detachment descended from the ridge. The family joined them; an aged woman Fraser took to be the grandmother hurrying over to embrace him fiercely.

'Gracias señor, gracias,' she kept repeating, before addressing the approaching riflemen. *'Gracias saltamontes!'*

Saltamontes, Fraser though. Grasshoppers. The nickname for the green-jacketed British riflemen.

'Tell them that they need to go,' Plunket told Fraser as he reached the gathering. 'That they should have left weeks ago. The French will be back. There'll be reprisals.'

Fraser passed on the information. The mother – her boy now gripped firmly to her skirt tails – began to say that they had nowhere to go, but her husband interrupted, telling Fraser that they would leave later that day, and thanking him again.

'Sorry I left it late, sir,' the rifleman from the rooftop said with a grin as he joined them. 'Wanted to be sure of the shot.'

'How did you get up there in the first place?' Fraser asked him.

'Funny what you can do when the shooting starts – everyone tends to get a bit distracted,' the man said.

'You've done this sort of thing before,' Fraser surmised, looking at Plunket.

'Someone has to remind the frogs there's a war on,' another of the riflemen, the man Fraser assumed was Jones, said. He had paused to strip the pockets of the slain dragoons on the way down the slope, but now caught up with his compatriots, tucking his loot away into his haversack as he came.

'Why does the duke want to see me?' Plunket interrupted bluntly, addressing Fraser. The lieutenant felt a sense of relief at the fact that he could finally address the reason he had sought the rifleman out in the first place.

'His Grace wishes to speak with you about a matter that has been brought to his attention. He instructed me to inform you that a single shot might make or break the entire war.'

Fraser had expected Plunket to at least be surprised, or intrigued, but the ragged rifleman just gave him a sour look. The others didn't appear much happier either.

'What've you done to piss them off this time?' Mackintosh asked Plunket. The rifleman just shrugged.

'This is an order, is it?' he asked Fraser.

'Yes. You are instructed to attend Third Division headquarters with me, immediately.'

For a horrifying moment, Fraser thought Plunket was going to refuse to do so, but after a short, cold silence, he slung his rifle across his shoulder.

'Lead on then,' he told him.

THE GREENJACKETS RETRIEVED their knapsacks, which they had left on the ridge, and Fraser went back to Bucephalus. After the surging excitement of the skirmish, he felt suddenly drained and awkward. It was clear Plunket didn't view a visit to headquarters as a positive thing, and that the riflemen had no wish to share his company on the journey there. They were hard, worn men, their uniforms patched and faded almost to brown, their shakos battered, their shoes threadbare. Their faces were lean and lined with care. Their rifles, however, were without any mark or blemish.

It wasn't long into their journey back towards the picket line that Fraser began to find the silence too painful to endure.

'Back at the farm, why did you shoot the horses and not the dragoons?' he asked Plunket eventually, thinking back to the skirmish.

'The range was too great to be sure of hitting one of the dragoons,' he said. 'Horses are easier targets, especially when they're hitched together. I just wanted to get their attention.'

'They might have killed that peasant family before you could fire again,' Fraser pointed out.

'How? There were too many for them to easily shoot, especially while they were coming under attack. Killing that family wasn't their priority, or they would have done it before we arrived.'

'They had swords.'

'Clearly you've never killed anyone with a sword,' Plunket replied, his tone dismissive. 'Messy, and not always quick.'

Unable to argue the point, Fraser lapsed back into silence for a while. The riflemen seemed content to walk without talking.

'Is it true at Cacabelos you shot two French generals at six hundred yards, one after the other?' Fraser asked as they neared the vineyard where he had encountered the British videttes earlier that afternoon.

This time Plunket said nothing, not even acknowledging the question. The other three riflemen laughed.

'Six hundred, is it now?' the Welshman, Jones, spoke up. 'How long before it's eight hundred, then a thousand?'

'Do you even know the range of a Baker rifle, lad?' Mackintosh asked.

'Three hundred yards, maximum?' Fraser ventured, feeling foolish.

'More like two hundred,' Mackintosh responded. 'Three hundred if you're a lucky bastard like the corporal here, and you're not trying to hit the same mark more than once in a row.'

'So, it was two hundred yards, not six hundred?' Fraser said. There was a short silence, the other riflemen looking at Plunket as he continued to trudge ahead. Fraser saw they were smirking, trying to goad the irascible corporal into responding.

'To hit and kill two generals one after the other at two hundred yards is still exceptional,' Fraser said, doing his best to recover the situation.

'It wasn't two generals,' Plunket finally called back, voice terse. 'It was one general. His name was Colbert. The second man was his aide. They never told me what his name was.'

There was a pause before Plunket added, 'And it was three hundred yards.'

The other riflemen jeered, and Fraser, despite himself, smiled.

Chapter Four

Outside Badajoz, Spain,
October 5th, 1809

It was getting dark when they arrived at Third Division headquarters. Plunket had left Smith, Mackintosh and Jones with the pickets, not wanting to get them involved. He had a grim feeling about what was waiting for him.

Lieutenant Fraser showed him into the commandeered farmhouse, leading him past the sentries and through a kitchen into what appeared to have been a dining area. Candles were lit, and there was a fire crackling in the grate, lending a brooding air to the gathering.

Plunket knew as soon as he entered the room that he was damned, as damned as the sinners the priest had preached about in the chapel when he was a young boy. Besides Fraser and another subaltern, there were three men waiting for him. One was Wellington himself, looking as lugubrious as ever, dressed in a dark blue jacket and seated at the head of the room's table, long fingers clasped over a scattering of maps, charts and papers. His grey eyes watched Plunket keenly as he entered.

On the duke's right was a heavyset figure in drab civilian attire, with a smile that made Plunket want to shiver. He had seen him at headquarters before, and had heard enough stories, especially among the 95th, to recognise him as one of the duke's spymasters, Simpson.

The last man present was Lieutenant Colonel Robertson, his dark green and black-faced rifleman's uniform helping him merge into the shadows of the room's far corner. Plunket caught his eye, Robertson's expression unreadable. As bad a portent as it was finding himself summoned in front of Wellington and someone like Simpson, it was Robertson's presence – as welcome as an undertaker at a wedding – that gave Plunket a plunging sense of foreboding.

He snapped to attention and saluted the duke.

'Corporal Plunket, 95th Rifles,' he barked. 'You wanted to see me, sir?'

Wellington returned the salute brusquely.

'At ease, man, at ease,' he said. 'Do you know Mister Simpson here?'

'I do not, sir,' Plunket said stoically, not looking at the spymaster.

'He… helps solve problems that others can't,' Wellington said carefully. 'And he has recently encountered a particular problem that you, apparently, are well-suited to assist him with.'

Plunket knew better than to speak his mind right away. He glanced at Simpson, and the rotund man gave him another deathly smile. Plunket didn't return it, instead fixing his attention on the far wall, adopting the unbending air of military rigidity he had always found helped smooth encounters with senior officers and their cabals.

'Ever heard of Zaragoza, Corporal Plunket?' Simpson asked when it became clear Plunket wasn't going to reply.

'Yes,' he said, refusing to address Simpson as "sir" even though he suspected the man held some technical rank. 'It's a town.'

'Know where it is?'

'Spain.'

If Plunket's lack of cooperation stung Simpson in any way, he gave no sign.

'Spain indeed. Far to the north-east of here. Almost four hundred and fifty miles, as the crow flies, which is of no use to you, unless you have wings furled and hidden under that green jacket of yours.'

Plunket didn't respond to the mockery, merely kept staring straight ahead.

'Do you know what the Leblanc Process is, Corporal Plunket?' Simpson went on.

'No, sir,' Plunket replied woodenly. Simpson smiled that death-smile again.

'Good. I become nervous around men who know more than me. I will spare you the details but suffice to say several decades ago a French chemist named Nicolas Leblanc invented a process whereby a component of gunpowder, soda ash, could be more easily produced using modern, industrial processes. The French revolutionary government forced him to reveal his formula to them and drove him to suicide. Now, their factories use the Leblanc Process to produce high-quality gunpowder at speeds no other nation in Europe can match.

'One such factory has recently been constructed on the edge of Zaragoza, under the supervision of a particularly brilliant chemist named Francois Dubertrand. For the past month, the place has been supplying the French armies throughout Iberia with vast quantities of munitions.'

'And what does this have to do with me?' Plunket asked, already suspecting he knew the answer, but wanting to drive Simpson to the point.

'Partisans local to the Zaragoza area believe they could inhibit the flow of gunpowder, perhaps even significantly damage the process, but they have requested support,' Simpson elaborated. 'Sending reinforcements to such a distant corner of Spain, through the heart of enemy territory, is far from feasible, but a more… covert strike is being discussed. His Grace wishes you to lead said strike. You, and a small number of your fellow riflemen. A section of three should do. You may pick them.'

'Four hundred and fifty miles, you say?' Plunket asked, finally looking Simpson in the eye. The ruddy little man smiled.

'As the crow flies.'

'Straight through the heart of enemy territory?'

'Just so.'

'Was it Lieutenant Colonel Robertson that volunteered me for this little jaunt, by any chance?' Plunket asked, looking from Simpson to his immediate superior. Robertson looked as though he were about to take issue with Plunket's tone but checked himself.

'Your reputation as the finest marksman in the entire army precedes you,' Simpson said. 'I have heard tell of what happened at Cacabelos, during the retreat to Corunna. Who has not? It is the popular opinion that, for accuracy, you can outshoot anyone on this part of the continent: British, Portuguese, Spanish or French.'

'Can't knock down factory walls with musket balls, no matter how well you shoot them,' Plunket said.

He knew he was being insubordinate, but it was detestable standing in front of such men – especially a parasite like Simpson – knowing he was being treated as nothing more than a wholly expendable pawn.

'Your role wouldn't be to destroy the factory itself,' Simpson said. 'Francois Dubertrand would be your target. The Leblanc Process formula is still closely guarded by French authorities, and Dubertrand is known to be particularly paranoid about such things. Removing him from the equation should be sufficient to curtail the factory's production for some months, at least. That will buy us time to work towards a more… permanent solution.'

'If that's the case, then I'll go alone,' Plunket said. 'Just me, and the partisans. No one else.'

'You'll take a section of three men,' Robertson said, reiterating Simpson's instructions.

'You want to get me killed, that's fair enough, sir, but I can't ask for any of the other lads to die with me,' Plunket said, holding Robertson's gaze fiercely.

'Now look here—' Robertson began to say, but Wellington interrupted him.

'Your summation of the situation is incorrect, corporal,' the general said, his tone as cold and cutting as ever. 'The circumstances might be difficult, yes, but they are necessary, and you are being sent with every hope of success. If you won't pick a trio of marksmen to accompany you, Lieutenant Colonel Robertson shall. Is that understood?'

The urge to damn the whole lot of them to hell was almost overwhelming, but Plunket channelled his anger and frustration into a loud, clear response.

'Yes, sir!'

'Very well,' Wellington said. 'You'll have tonight to choose them and get some rest. Simpson will see you off in the morning, with the final specifics. Once you've met the partisans, you can get on your way.'

Plunket neither moved nor spoke, and Wellington raised an eyebrow.

'Is there something more, corporal?'

'Well, sir, if you want me to ride with the Spaniards, things might get more than a little unfortunate if I don't speak their lingo, which I don't. I could use a translator, preferably one of our own, so I know I can trust them.'

Wellington grunted and glanced briefly at Simpson before speaking.

'A fair point, I suppose. I'm sure Mister Simpson will be able to furnish you with someone appropriate.'

'A British officer?' Plunket asked doubtfully, not wanting to find himself saddled with one of the spymaster's dubious informers or some local brigand.

'I'll go,' said a voice before Simpson could respond. All

eyes turned to the subaltern who had just spoken – it was the one who had ridden beyond the lines to fetch Plunket, the fresh-faced youth in scarlet called Lieutenant Fraser.

'I believe I might be of some use,' the young officer went on hastily, blanching now that he was suddenly the centre of attention. 'I… well, I speak fluent Spanish, so it would be remiss if I didn't volunteer my services.'

'You are a member of my staff, Mister Fraser,' Wellington said sternly. 'Your services are at my disposal. They are not yours to volunteer.'

'My apologies, sir,' Fraser said, his pallid complexion rapidly beginning to turn a similar shade to his coat. 'But I thought it would be ill of me if I did not speak up.'

'And what would the good Reverend Fraser think when he discovers I have sent his son off into the wilderness with only a handful of riflemen and an unknown band of Spanish ruffians?' Wellington pointed out.

'I believe he would be proud that I am doing my duty, sir,' Fraser said.

'Your duty is here,' Wellington began to growl, but Simpson interjected.

'If I might offer an opinion, Lieutenant Fraser may well be an apt candidate for this role,' he said. 'The Spanish are unlikely to be thrilled that our support consists of only four riflemen, even if one is the famed Corporal Plunket. Including a red-coated officer may help… prove our good intentions.'

'You're saying they wouldn't think you'd let the boy join us if you were sure we're all to be killed,' Plunket said.

'I'm ready to take on an equal share of the danger if it means striking a blow against Bonaparte,' Fraser said defiantly.

Plunket decided that telling him only a fool would volunteer for a task like this would be a waste of breath. He'd seen enough of the boy to know there wasn't a great deal going on between his ears other than youthful exuberance.

The duke was no longer attempting to mask his exasperation with cold indifference.

'Very well then, Fraser, if your mind is made up,' he snapped. 'You will join Corporal Plunket's expedition.'

Fraser grinned briefly before adopting a more suitably guarded expression.

'Thank you, sir,' he said. 'I won't let you down.'

'You are both dismissed,' Wellington declared, already picking up a pen and dipping its nib in an ink well set next to him, before drawing a fresh sheaf of documents across the desk towards him.

Plunket and Fraser saluted and made to depart, but the duke's voice checked them at the doorway.

'The army is in a precarious state, Corporal Plunket,' he called out. 'The gunpowder this *Monsieur* Dubertrand is producing will be directly responsible for the deaths of hundreds, maybe thousands of our men if used against us. Your comrades in arms, and mine. So, if you won't do this for me, or for Robertson here, then do it for your fellows in green and in red. Go and kill me that damned chemist.'

Plunket looked back at the duke. Then, wordlessly, he nodded and left.

THAT EVENING, PLUNKET rounded up Mackintosh, Smith and Jones, and told them the bad news.

'I'm not asking you to come with me,' he said as he sat with them around the mess campfire, gazing at them through the flames. 'But I'd rather have you three than any other bastards Robertson might pick.'

'He's going to be the death of the lot of us,' Jones grumbled as he pulled his ramrod free from his rifle's barrel, the wet cloth wrapped around its tip black now with gunpowder fouling.

'That's my fault, and no one else's,' Plunket admitted. 'And that's why you shouldn't be coming. But I wanted to let you all know.'

The four lapsed into contemplative silence. While Jones finished cleaning his rifle, the others were working their way through the meagre bowls of stew they had scooped out of the mess kettle bubbling over the fire. Food was scarce along the Guadiana, but it was still a damn sight better than the rations they had endured in the past, especially during the retreat through Galicia at the start of the year. That was a hunger Plunket had only known twice before – once, when the crops had failed in his home county of Wexford, and the second time in a Spanish prison on the other side of the world. Compared to those hardships, a half-full kettle with scraps of stringy goat and peas and a loaf of stale bread felt like a feast.

'I'm minded to come with you,' Mackintosh spoke up eventually. 'But only because you've the luck of the Irish, and knowing you, you'll be back here in a month's time with more tall tales for us all to endure. They'll have you back up to sergeant by the end of the year.'

'And then stripped back down to corporal even faster, next time you step out of line,' Smith laughed.

'If you couldn't shoot the way you do, they'd have flogged you to death by now,' Jones added, unwrapping the cloth from his ramrod and returning the steel tool to the brass loops underneath his rifle's barrel.

'The army finds me useful, so I need to keep being useful,' Plunket admitted. 'But it's not on your heads. None of you need to come.'

'We're as likely to meet a miserable end here as we are going on your little jaunt,' Jones pointed out. 'Peters and Doleman died last night. The fever. Even the lieutenant is down with it. The whole bloody army's sick.'

'It's a bad place for winter quarters,' Smith agreed. 'Place is festering with disease. You should have told the duke that when you had his ear.'

'Think you might be misunderstanding how our conversation went,' Plunket said with a dry laugh. 'But I've let you lads know what I'll be about. God willing I'll be seeing you all again before Christmas. If not, well, make sure no one else but one of you three takes the top regimental marksmanship score. I'll haunt the whole damn pack of you if that bastard Williams takes it.'

'Stop playing so coy, you bloody Paddy,' Mackintosh exclaimed, the firelight dancing over his grin. 'We're not sitting here while you have all the fun. We're with you, aren't we, lads?'

The other two riflemen nodded.

'Why not?' Jones said. 'Better than sitting here rotting away all winter. From the sounds of it the frogs will blow us to kingdom come when spring arrives anyway.'

'And it gets us away from Robertson and the like,' Smith pointed out.

Plunket felt a surge of relief he did his best to mask. It was an unworthy emotion, he knew. He was asking his mess mates – the only friends he really had – to risk their lives. If he were a stronger man, a better man, he would have met Simpson the next morning and told him no one else was coming, and if he didn't like it then he could go to the devil and ask him to find another marksman.

But the duke's words rang true. Plunket didn't give a damn about the schemes of rats like Simpson, but if the French really were on the cusp of unleashing hell through a chemist and his factory, then Plunket knew there would be no avoiding it. Sometimes, just as at the bridge at Cacabelos, the best hope was to take the initiative.

Sometimes, it was better to strike first.

Chapter Five

Fort Josephine, Zaragoza, North-Eastern Spain,
October 6th, 1809

THE THIEF'S NAME, according to one of the guards who recognised him, was Paolo.

'Ask Paolo who told him to steal this,' Francois Dubertrand demanded of Major d'Arcy, brandishing the papers he had just retrieved from the prisoner.

Guillame d'Arcy asked the question of Paolo, in Spanish. The factory worker's expression remained sullen, and his eyes darted from the guards holding him, to Dubertrand and then to d'Arcy, but he otherwise showed no indication of having understood what had just been said.

'He is feigning ignorance,' d'Arcy told Dubertrand.

Outside, a bell rang the hour, signalling a shift change at the factory. The chimes reached up through the window into the drawing room of the villa Dubertrand had claimed as his office. The handsome stone structure was one of the few buildings still standing within the earthworks and bastions recently christened Fort Josephine.

Dubertrand let out a little hissing sound through the gap between his front teeth, as d'Arcy found he was wont to do when annoyed, which seemed to be often. He was a tall, bony and erratic man, young but appearing older, with a mess of silvering hair crammed under a tall, lean top-hat whose beaver pelt had seen better days. His clothing – a shabby black suit and white cravat – seemed to hang from his frame, like example pieces over a wrong-sized mannequin in a draper's shop. Most curious of all were his hands, his long, clutching fingers seemingly perpetually stained with strange shades of black, blue and purple, the results, d'Arcy assumed, of excessive chemical experimentation.

He was not a military man by any sense of the word, which only made d'Arcy's circumstances – a major in the French army, seconded to this strange civilian – even more privately lamentable.

'He cannot possibly comprehend the importance of these formulas,' Dubertrand went on in French, speaking to d'Arcy while carefully putting each piece of paper he had retrieved back into the desk drawer the intruder had broken into. 'He is a filthy, dull-brained Spanish peasant! That means someone must have told him what to look for when he came in here. Someone who understands the value of my work!'

'I suspect the factory labourers are less ignorant than you might believe, monsieur,' d'Arcy said carefully. 'Production has been proceeding for some months, and news of your… breakthroughs are undoubtedly spreading.'

Dubertrand did not seem to be listening – he was readjusting a small marble bust that had been knocked over during the struggle to detain Paolo. When he had first met d'Arcy, he had lectured him at length about the identity of the bust, the great French chemist Antoine-Laurent de Lavoisier. D'Arcy had heard of him – his father, a man of the Enlightenment, had done his best to inculcate him with both a classical and humanist education – but Dubertrand's claims that he had studied under Lavoisier and was his favourite student and confidant, seemed hard to believe.

'Look how this peasant has disturbed my desk,' Dubertrand said as he finished carefully placing the bust. 'That alone is an offence warranting a capital punishment.'

D'Arcy could not tell if he was joking.

'I will question the prisoner further about his motives and accomplices,' he told Dubertrand. The chemist waved a hand, frowning.

'No, no, this rat won't talk. He must be made an example of, as swiftly as possible. Executed, Major!'

'But you just said you wanted to discover if he—'

'You are distracting me, Major d'Arcy! This little fracas has put me behind schedule, and that is not something we can afford! The emperor demands results, and I intend to deliver them!'

'You wish the prisoner shot, then?' d'Arcy said, determined to pin down the chemist's orders. They had clashed about these kinds of matters – from the treatment of the factory labourers to the purging of suspected partisans and malcontents within the workforce – too many times. In the months since the chemist had been given authority over Fort Josephine, he had systematically turned the French army garrison into his own private thugs. It disgusted d'Arcy, but he had no leeway for complaints. He knew his assignment to the forces occupying Zaragoza had been a calculated punishment by senior commanders, inflicted on him because of his outspoken opposition to the wider tactics being used to combat the hated guerrillas.

'Shoot him, hang him, drown him. Do whatever it is you soldiers do when you catch a spy.'

'When we catch a spy, the first thing we do is put them on trial.'

Dubertrand snorted mockingly.

'Spy is too grand a word for this vermin. Now get him out of my sight. I have lost enough time to this as it is!'

D'Arcy nodded to the guards, and they heaved Paolo towards the door. The Spaniard finally spoke up, spitting a series of invectives at Dubertrand, which the chemist ignored.

'At least this latest incident will prove to General Girard that the garrison needs to be reinforced,' he said to d'Arcy. 'And the workers must be checked again! The partisans infest everything here!'

'I will speak to the general as soon as possible,' d'Arcy said.

'Today,' Dubertrand pressed. 'And I want this thieving rat hung before sunset as well! That will send a message to whoever sent him.'

D'Arcy considered reiterating that the prisoner should be tried first, but he knew it would do no good. Dubertrand was already starting to feverishly scribble on a fresh sheaf of papers, the scratching of his pen replacing the noise of the prisoner being dragged away.

Saying nothing, d'Arcy let himself out.

The riflemen left with the dawn.

Simpson had come and found them beforehand and furnished them with maps and instructions on where the guerillas were waiting for them, but he had provided no written orders. Plunket had protested – if they were taken, he said, there was every chance they might be executed out of hand if they could not prove they were soldiers acting on the instructions of their superiors.

'Do as the duke's exploring officers do, and keep your uniform on at all times,' Simpson had advised. 'If you're taken in uniform, the rules of war must apply.'

Plunket told Simpson exactly what he thought about the probability of the rules of war being applied in his case, but the spymaster didn't seem to care. He bade them good fortune and the joy of the hunt, and left them at the picket line, riding back into the darkness.

The four riflemen departed, accompanied by Lieutenant Fraser. The young officer had joined them on the edge of the camp, wearing a grey greatcoat to ward off the morning chill. After his excitement yesterday, he was clearly nervous, his face white amidst the dawn's pale shades. Plunket said nothing to him, other than to repeat the words he had uttered when they had first met the day before.

'Do exactly as I say, when I say.'

At least the boy appeared happy enough to follow orders, despite his technically superior rank. There was nothing worse than an arrogant young pup of an officer, and the British army in Spain had plenty of those.

The riflemen moved out at a quick pace, all four of them on foot while Fraser rode behind. Simpson had claimed the partisans would furnish them with mounts once they had made contact.

The sun rose, and Plunket settled into a familiar rhythm. Hard marching came just as easily to experienced light infantry as hard fighting, and a part of Plunket was relieved to be on the move again after weeks spent festering along the fever-ridden Guadiana.

The new day revealed a hard, autumnal landscape of craggy hills and small fields and vineyards, the trees in the process of shedding their golden-brown canopies. There were few signs of life in the hamlets and farmsteads they passed by – this was the contested ground between the two armies, a place made desolate by the shifting pace of the war through central Spain. A few people gazed warily at them as they passed by from behind walls or windows, closing doors and locking shutters as they approached.

There were no signs of the French that morning, but about an hour before midday Jones, taking his turn walking a little way ahead of the small group, called back.

'Rider on the ridge, to the right.'

Plunket had already spotted the figure. They had been attempting to keep back from the crest, but the sun was silhouetting them. It made it impossible to be sure of their identity, but Plunket didn't think they had a helmet on, which made it less likely it was a French cavalryman.

'Keep going,' he instructed the others.

They passed into a rocky valley, the sounds of their feet scraping on the pathway echoing back from its steep sides. The rider followed them at a distance, stalking them for perhaps a mile, before vanishing as swiftly as they had appeared.

'Who do you think he was?' Fraser said, sounding nervous.

'I suspect we're about to find out,' Plunket responded, as he caught the clattering sounds of more hooves.

Horsemen appeared, a dozen this time, cantering out from the cover of a rocky outcrop to cut off their route through the valley. More emerged behind them, all dressed in rough civilian garments. Some were men, some were women, but all were armed, sporting a mismatched array of muskets, sabres and repurposed farming tools.

'Easy, lads,' Plunket said quietly, bringing their advance to a halt, cradling his rifle in his arms. 'Half cock, fingers off the triggers.'

He shot a warning glance at Fraser in particular, whose hand had started to stray towards his sword's hilt.

'I hope your Spanish is still as good as it was yesterday,' he told him. 'Draw back that greatcoat while you're at it. Let's make it nice and obvious who we are.'

The lieutenant swallowed and opened up his greatcoat to show the smart scarlet and gold uniform underneath.

The riders closed in. Plunket fixed his eyes on the one at the front, stepping forward to meet him. He was a tall man on a fine-looking horse, his upper body wrapped in a striped poncho, with a broad-brimmed hat throwing his moustachioed face into shadow.

The horsemen halted in front of them, and the two parties surveyed one another, Plunket trying to get the measure of their leader while giving nothing away. He glanced at Fraser and gestured for him to come forward.

'Introduce us,' he told the lieutenant. 'And ask them if these are the partisans we've been looking for.'

'We are,' the lead horseman said in English, before Fraser could speak. Though his shadowed expression remained stolid, there was a gleam of amusement in his dark eyes as he went on. 'And you are the Englishmen your Mister Simpson promised us? All five of you?'

Plunket decided that now wasn't the time to point out that, technically, the only member of the expedition who was actually English was Rifleman Smith.

'We are,' he said instead.

'You command here, or him?' the partisan asked, gesturing curtly from Plunket to Fraser. 'I see one man in scarlet, on a horse, and I see another in dirty green rags, on foot, and the answer seems obvious, but only at a distance, yes?'

'Mister Fraser here is an officer, and I am not,' Plunket said, with more care than he was used to.

Now, the partisan's mirth spread beyond his eyes. He let out a short, rich chuckle.

'Do not worry, I understand. In Spain, our own army is not so different, and I think it is the same the world over. My son here, Carlos, is a lieutenant in the *Ejército de Tierra*.'

He gestured at the partisan to his immediate left, a young man with bristling sideburns who gazed fiercely down at Plunket.

'But Carlos knows that when Sergeant Hernández says to do something, it must be done,' he carried on, now gesturing to the man on his right, a short, stocky figure on an equally short, stocky horse, one side of his face scarred by the brutal puckering of a spent musket ball.

'Officers command, but it is men like you and Hernández who lead, is it not?' the partisan finished, giving Plunket a knowing smile.

'You are soldiers then, not partisans?' Plunket asked, not wishing to be drawn in by casual conversation. The man shrugged.

'Not all of us,' he said. 'Most are honest labourers and farmhands who have suffered too much, and who have seen their families suffer too much. But yes, my sergeant and my son here served with me in the *Ejército de Cataluña*, with the army of His Most Catholic Majesty. And we serve still, though our regiment is no more. My name is Captain Ferdinand Martinez El Cruz, and these men and women are as much my soldiers as any in the old regiment. And you four, you are English riflemen, are you not? *Saltamontes*.'

Plunket nodded, and El Cruz laughed again.

'Yes, I know those green coats. The French know them, too, and fear them. What I wouldn't give, to have just six of those short rifles you carry in the hands of my best marksmen. You English give out gold and guns to the guerillas, but not your rifles.'

'If we gave out rifles as well, I'd be putting myself out of a job,' Plunket said.

El Cruz seemed to take a moment to understand, then grinned.

'What is your name, *saltamontes*?' he asked.

'Corporal Thomas Plunket, of the 95th,' Plunket replied.

Immediately, El Cruz's expression changed. Gone was the mirth, replaced by a sudden darkness. He spoke sharply in Spanish to the short man next to him, his sergeant. The man responded with what sounded like an affirmative and, glaring at Plunket, spat on the ground.

'What did he just say?' Plunket demanded of Fraser.

'The captain, uh, he asked something about your name,' Fraser mumbled.

'Damn it, do you speak Spanish or not?' Plunket snapped.

'Is this some form of joke by your Lord Wellington?' El Cruz asked, this time speaking to Fraser.

'It is not a joke, sir,' Fraser said stiffly, clearly perplexed. 'If you're referring to the fact that there are only five of us, I can assure you these riflemen are some of the best soldiers in the British Army. Corporal Plunket here is the hero of Cacabelos.'

'I know who Corporal Plunket is,' El Cruz said acidly. He spoke more words to his assembled men, and wheeled away with a group of them, moving a short distance along the valley to converse out of earshot from Fraser.

'What's this all about?' Fraser asked nervously. None of the riflemen responded.

Plunket had been afraid something like this would happen. There was nothing he could do, no action he could now take that would change the past or redeem him in the eyes of men like these Spaniards, or Lieutenant Colonel Robertson.

Eventually, El Cruz and his subordinates returned.

'My son believes that we should abandon this venture right away, and send you back to your Lord Wellington, after taking those rifles as recompense for the wastage of our time,' he told the British. The young man he had introduced earlier nodded gravely, as El Cruz went on.

'But I am a forgiving man, and a practical one. We know that God works in mysterious ways, and that is why he has sent the likes of you to aid us. Regardless of what has happened in the past, my dear people suffer in the present under the hand of a foreign invader, and anyone who wishes to drive that invader from my home, I will accept as an ally.'

Plunket nodded, supposing he couldn't hope for better than that. For a while, he had feared the partisans would turn on them outright.

'To Zaragoza, then,' he said, slinging his rifle over his shoulder.

'To Zaragoza,' El Cruz agreed.

Chapter Six

Along the Guadiana, Spain,
October 6th, 1809

THE PARTISANS PROVIDED mounts for the four riflemen, and they rode east.

Fraser was still trying to make sense of the encounter as darkness fell, and they took to a small plateau to encamp for the night. Plunket was saying as little as ever, while the other three riflemen had only muttered amongst themselves during the ride. Fraser felt as though he was the only one, British or Spanish, who didn't understand the dynamic of the group since Plunket had told the Spaniards his name. It made him nervous.

'Does Captain El Cruz know Corporal Plunket?' Fraser said eventually to Jones, as he stepped away from the other greenjackets to refill their canteens at the brook running along the plateaux's northern edge.

'Not personally, no,' Jones said, giving Fraser an unfriendly glance.

'Why the discord then? His whole attitude changed when Plunket said his name,' Fraser pressed.

'Spaniards can be funny like that sometimes,' Jones said, stooping over to dunk the first canteen in the stream.

'I'm not sure that's the case,' Fraser said, at which the rifleman straightened up, looking at him hard.

'With all due respect, sir, if you want to know about those sorts of things, you're best asking the corporal yourself.'

Fraser resisted the urge to tell the man he was being insubordinate – he knew that kind of view would do him no favours out here. He couldn't afford to alienate anyone on the expedition, let alone the four riflemen. Yet at the same time, not understanding why the Spanish were so set against Plunket felt intolerable.

'What about Lieutenant Colonel Robertson?' Fraser asked, deciding to change the angle of attack. 'What happened between him and Plunket?'

'It were before my time,' Jones began to say, then checked himself, kneeling back down with the next canteen.

'If the corporal wants you to know, he'll tell you,' he said. 'Before then, I'd say let it rest, sir. For your own sake as much as his.'

'IN A RIGHT bind here, aren't we?' Mackintosh murmured to Plunket as they watched the autumn sun set. Smith was setting up a small lean-to against some rocks using torn-up shrubbery and branches, while Jones had been sent off to refill the canteens. Plunket didn't know what had become of Fraser, but suspected he was badgering Jones. He refused to allow himself to feel responsible for the boy. He shouldn't have come.

'Do you trust them?' Mackintosh continued, referring to the partisans creating their own rudimentary camp a short distance away. The riflemen had agreed that no campfires would be lit – the area they were in was supposedly still free of the French, but there was no sense in drawing attention on their first night.

'We've no choice but to trust them while we're out here,' Plunket admitted. 'This is their country, and this whole expedition was their idea. If they wanted to kill us tonight, they could.'

'Not without losing a few of their own during the effort.' Mackintosh grinned viciously. 'Think El Cruz was out there in the Americas at the same time as we were?'

'Doesn't matter, does it?' Plunket said, not wanting to have that conversation. It was just one more mess on top of all the others.

He fished into his knapsack and drew out his pewter pipe and tobacco pouch.

'Get some food down you, then sleep,' he instructed Mackintosh and Smith, noticing Jones returning with the canteens and a forlorn-looking Fraser in tow. 'I'll take the first watch.'

THE NIGHT WAS an uneasy one. Plunket patrolled the western edge of the plateau, hunting the shadows for any signs of threat while remaining conscious of the guards the guerillas had posted also moving in the dark. The moon was high and bright, the sky clear, the air cold.

He tried not to let his thoughts wander, tried not to think about the damnable mess he had managed to work his way into, again. Most importantly, he tried not to think about how he was endangering the lives of the only men he knew he could count on as friends.

But there was nothing he could do about any of that, not now. Orders were orders. That was an excuse, he knew, but at least it was a familiar one.

He paused on his route along the southern length of the slope, listening. Were those voices he had caught the sound of? Yes, but not from ahead, from behind, back up the slope. Words being exchanged in low, hissed tones, in Spanish.

Treading carefully, Plunket moved towards the sound. He was close to the southern side of where the guerillas were encamped, at the limit of the route he'd been patrolling. Whoever the speakers were, they had walked away from their own camp to converse in private.

Plunket stood still again and strained his eyes in the dark, catching motion in the moonlight. Two figures close to a skeletal tree, their exact identities difficult to tell.

He remained where he was, trying to discern individual words, wondering if he would be able to glean any sort of meaning from them at all.

The conversation grew more heated. It was a man and a woman, he realised. The words meant nothing to him, but whatever they were saying, it wasn't cordial. Eventually the woman spat something and swept away in the direction of the camp.

The other figure lingered and looked about. Plunket remained still, silent, wondering if the Spaniard had sensed him. He thought he had recognised the voice, though he wasn't entirely certain.

Muttering under his breath, the second figure eventually also began to climb up towards the partisan camp.

Plunket watched him go then, after a while listening to the silence that followed, resumed his patrol.

GENERAL GIRARD RECEIVED Major d'Arcy in his headquarters, overlooking the soaring structure of the Church of Santa Engracia de Zaragoza.

Word had come early in the day, requesting d'Arcy's presence before the commander of the Zaragoza garrison. He had left Fort Josephine without even informing Dubertrand that he would be absent, in no mood to deal with the vile man that morning.

Zaragoza was still suffering, and d'Arcy was reminded of its pain as he rode through the ruins of its streets. Nowhere in Spain had resisted the French occupation more violently. For almost three months, from December through to late February that year, Spanish soldiers and civilians had entrenched themselves within the town and fought to defend it with utter ferocity. The siege had resulted in the deaths of around ten thousand French soldiers, almost thirty thousand Spanish troops, and over thirty thousand townsfolk, a ravaging they had seemed willing to pay, if it meant resisting the invaders. They had likened it to a religious crusade, their priests and nuns firing the populace to defiance, urging them to defend the sanctity of their homes to the last. The Spanish had fought street by street, house by house, before the survivors had finally been compelled to surrender to a French army fifty thousand strong.

D'Arcy had not witnessed the terrible siege, though he had heard the stories, and witnessed the aftermath. He had arrived nearly a month after the town's conquest, yet even then they had not finished burying all the dead.

So much for the concept that d'Arcy knew some of his fellow officers clung to, the belief that the revolution in their homeland was the beginning of a new age, a new dawn for humanity where quaint concepts like religion and fealty to royal crowns were relegated to the dusty cupboard of posterity.

If the French were bringing forth a new age, it was not one the Spanish wanted any part in.

The burned-out buildings and ruined walls d'Arcy passed were a sombre reflection of that, but in truth simply being out of Fort Josephine was a relief. It felt as though he had escaped from Dubertrand's grasp. The chemist's shadow had been left behind, if only temporarily. To the credit of General Girard, he all-but refused to treat with Dubertrand, and would only communicate with Fort Josephine's garrison through his fellow-officer, d'Arcy.

At headquarters, one of the general's aides ushered him inside and led him up to Girard's office. The room overlooked the Church of Santa Engracia de Zaragoza, a grand building that had played host to some of the bloodiest fighting during the siege. The piled rubble and scaffolding that still surrounded it marked the ongoing, months-long efforts to repair the havoc wreaked upon the heart of the town.

D'Arcy stepped fully into the drawing room, glancing first at the eagle of one of the French garrison regiments stood in the corner, its golden wings dull in the shadows, then up at the print of Napoleon gazing reproachfully down upon him from the opposite wall.

Girard was more welcoming than their emperor. He rose from behind his desk in front of the window, returned d'Arcy's salute, then came round and embraced him, planting a swift kiss on each cheek. The commander of the Zaragoza garrison was an old soldier, too old by most standards for hard campaigning, but considered a safe and level-headed appointment when it came to governing a recently conquered, rebellious town. He sympathised with d'Arcy, especially with his reasons for being relegated to Fort Josephine. They were both professionals and respected one another for it.

'How do you fare, my friend?' Girard asked, having him sit before reclaiming his own seat behind the desk.

'Well enough in body, if not in spirit,' d'Arcy admitted, knowing he could speak openly to the general. 'My charge grows more erratic by the day.'

'What has the chemist done now?' Girard asked patiently.

'He had me execute a man caught stealing papers from his office. He was likely a partisan, but there was no recourse to due process. Dubertrand demanded he be killed out of hand.'

'And has the sentence been carried out?'

'Yes, the very next morning, to my shame. I find myself assigned to this place because I would not bend the rules of war before, and yet here I am, being required to do so once again.'

'The exigencies of the service,' Girard said carefully. D'Arcy knew the general shared his distaste for Dubertrand, as much for the fact that senior officers were being required by the emperor's writ to subordinate themselves to a civilian, as for the fact the civilian in question was a brute. Yet orders were orders, and d'Arcy had no wish to put Girard in an uncomfortable position by goading him into speaking ill of those who commanded them, including the emperor.

'I am thankful for a little time away from the fort,' d'Arcy said, deciding it was best to move on. 'But I'm also eager to know why you've requested my attendance, sir.'

'I wish it were for nothing besides a long-overdue, cordial discussion, my friend,' Girard said, sorting through the papers on his desk until he found one envelope in particular, its seal broken. 'Unfortunately, I have asked you here to address a far more pressing matter.'

The general leaned across the table and d'Arcy reached out to accept the proffered envelope. He opened it.

'Word has arrived from an outside source, an individual loyal to France,' Girard said. 'And it is only right that I should inform you. I fear that very soon yourself and the garrison of Fort Josephine, as well as the upstanding Monsieur Dubertrand, will be in very grave danger.'

Chapter Seven

Near Talarrubias, Spain,
October 11th, 1809

THE JOURNEY CONTINUED the next day without interruption. The expedition held its eastward course, aiming to stay well south of Toledo and the River Tagus. Everything to the north of that point was controlled by the French, especially around Madrid, a city that Napoleon himself had conquered the year before. The route the partisans were taking was designed to circle east and avoid the main concentrations of the emperor's forces.

On the fifth day, they stopped on the outskirts of a village called Talarrubias, sleeping in a tavern and its adjacent barn. Two of the partisans got drunk on cheap wine, and El Curz's son, Carlos, responded by screaming at them the next morning in front of the entire expedition, until El Cruz intervened.

'The captain is telling him they aren't soldiers, and they can't be expected to behave like soldiers,' Fraser translated quietly for Plunket as the partisan leader berated his son in turn. 'He says they will be given another chance.'

'They're in no worse state than most of the lads were during the retreat to Corunna,' Mackintosh quipped.

Fraser resisted the urge to ask the rifleman about that. He had not been present during the infamous retreat, but he had heard the stories. Unimaginable privation had created a bond that he could never share in. It was just another difference widening the gulf he felt between himself and the riflemen.

He was still thinking about such matters when, later that day, he saw Carlos ride up alongside Plunket.

'Englishman,' he said by way of greeting, the words sounding more like an accusation.

'I'm Irish,' Plunket responded, but Carlos didn't seem to understand.

'You were in Buenos Aires, yes?' the Spaniard went on.

'Yes,' Plunket said stoically. Carlos turned away from him and spat, before saying something to him in quick-fire Spanish, too fast for Fraser to catch properly. Plunket simply glared at him, and Mackintosh rode up from behind, driving his horse between the two and keeping them apart.

'Carlos, *déjalo*,' barked El Cruz from the head of the column. Giving Plunket another withering stare, Carlos kicked his horse away from the British to join his father, the angry conversation that followed out of Fraser's earshot.

Buenos Aires. Fraser hadn't heard the place mentioned in relation to Plunket before. He knew nothing about it, other than the fact a British expeditionary force that had included the 95th Rifles had fought there two years before. The temptation to ask was almost overwhelming, but Fraser made himself bite his tongue. It would do no good to further annoy Plunket in the aftermath of the clash with Carlos, even if the reason for it was beyond Fraser.

THAT EVENING, THEY halted in a small woodland west of a place called Las Mesas. El Cruz permitted the partisans to light a fire, so Plunket let his men do the same. Fraser and the riflemen still hadn't shared so much as a meal with the Spaniards, keeping their own company each night. Plunket assumed that evening would be the same, until a figure approached the flames the British were huddled around. It was El Cruz.

'A little something to help keep the cold at bay,' the Spaniard said, drawing back his poncho to reveal a dark bottle of wine. He proffered it to Plunket, who made no move to accept it.

'I wish to apologise for what my son said earlier,' El Cruz went on.

'He could have been praising me to high heaven,' Plunket said, his tone surly. 'Didn't understand a bloody word of it.'

'That is for the best, then,' El Cruz said with a slender smile. 'Carlos is a headstrong young man. Who among us was not, at his age? I had hoped sending him away when he was a boy, giving him a good education, would tame the fire that burns in my family's soul. Three years studying in Paris, before the war, filled his head with philosophies, but the fire remains. I should just be thankful he is not as ferocious as his sister.'

'There's more of you?' Plunket asked, not really wanting to be drawn into conversation.

'Maria,' El Cruz said, carefully placing the bottle down next to Plunket when it became obvious he wasn't going to take it, but not moving to sit. 'She rides with us as well. I thought to tame her by making her take orders, in Zaragoza. Another mistake. She had barely started to wear the habit when the French burned the convent. Now she hates man, and God, and everything in between. I am starting to fear my family is cursed.'

'Your fault for having children,' Plunket said. El Cruz shrugged.

'They make life difficult, yes, but they also make it worth living. And they teach me, even if they do not realise, or mean to. They teach me how to forgive, and how to compromise.'

Plunket looked down at the bottle but said nothing.

'We turn north in two days' time,' El Cruz went on.

'Another eight days, maybe nine, and we will be in the vicinity of Zaragoza. I hope by then, we will have figured out a way of working together.'

'We won't need to work together,' Plunket said, not caring if there was venom in his voice. 'Show me that French chemist, and I'll show you a dead man.'

'We both know it won't be that simple,' El Cruz responded. 'They have built a fort around the factory, and he never leaves it. There is a large, dedicated garrison. Cavalry sweep the countryside around the town. You will need us if you are to get that chemist in your sights.'

'Then we'll talk about it all when we're closer,' Plunket said. 'Until then, keep your men away from mine. Especially Carlos. I don't need to speak Spanish to understand he doesn't know what he's talking about.'

'As you wish, *señor*,' El Cruz said, sounding disappointed with the outcome of his peace offering. He withdrew.

'Want me to save it for the return journey?' Mackintosh asked, eyeing the wine bottle. 'Or ration it out into the canteens?'

'Ration it out and dilute it into the water,' Plunket said, knowing better than to waste liquids. 'If we make it back, I'll make sure we've all got something stronger to drink.'

He sat back, and gazed into the fire, and thought about El Cruz, Maria and Carlos. The clash with the partisan leader's son had brought about an unexpected benefit, one he had yet to share with anyone else – he had recognised the Spaniard's voice. Carlos was the man he had overheard on the first night, arguing with a woman in the darkness on the edge of camp. And if anyone had offered it as a wager, he would have laid money on the woman in question being his sister, Maria.

Thoughts still turning, Plunket closed his eyes and waited for sleep to creep up on him.

Chapter Eight

Near Castillo de Peracense, North-Eastern Spain,
October 21st, 1809

THREE DAYS SOUTH of Zaragoza, El Cruz requested that the British join him in the barn he had taken up residence in for the night. For the past few days, the expedition had returned to sleeping outside without fires, but the structure allowed El Cruz to light a few candles without risk of giving away their presence. The illumination was necessary for what he intended to show the British.

'Tomorrow, Carlos will ride ahead and inform our allies within Zaragoza that we are close,' he told them. 'The time has come to discuss what we intend to do when we reach the town.'

A hay bale had been slung into the barn's centre, and several maps spread across it. Cattle scraped and lowed in the stalls nearby. The place stank of dung and damp. The candlelight flickered, barely strong enough to pick out the features of those gathered around – Fraser and the riflemen, as well as several of El Cruz's subordinates, including Carlos, his sergeant, Hernández, and a young woman Plunket took to be the daughter he had spoken of, Maria. She was paler and fairer than her father and brother, her expression grave and suspicious. She watched the British intently.

'I need to know everything I can about Dubertrand's movements,' Plunket replied to El Cruz. 'Where he eats, where he sleeps, where he works.'

'He never leaves Fort Josephine,' El Cruz said, tapping one of the maps. 'It was built here, on the western edge of the town, specifically to protect their new factory by the river.'

He drew another map across the first, this one cruder than the others, pencilled in. 'Getting inside is extremely difficult, but I have people among the workforce. They are made to live within the fort, but if they are sick, they are permitted to leave, probably to stop it spreading to the others. Food is also brought in, and spoil from the factory taken out and dumped.'

Plunket leaned over the bale, assessing the drawing. It showed a typical five-pointed bastion fort, hard on the banks of the river that ran through Zaragoza, the Ebro. It was the structures within the fort that drew his eye.

'What're these?' he asked El Cruz, indicating them.

'This is the main factory building,' the partisan replied, tapping each depiction in turn. 'And the workhouses next to it. This is a villa that stood on the site before the fort was built, it's where Dubertrand lives. These are the barracks and garrison stables, and this here was once a church. It was burned during the fighting at the start of the year, but the French haven't pulled down the remains yet. There are magazines and storehouses built into the redoubts and underground, and a covered way leading down to the jetty, here—'

He indicated where the fort's edge met the River Ebro, an opening in the defences giving access to the waterway.

'The initial loads of gunpowder were transported out of the fort via the river,' he went on. 'Barges carry the cargo along the Ebro. It's faster and safer than transporting it all by road.'

'Tell me about the church,' Plunket said. 'Does it have a tower?'

'It does, though how much inside still stands, I do not know,' El Cruz replied. 'The fire gutted it.'

'What about the factory, is the main structure tall?'

'The tallest in the fort, yes. Part of the roof is flat.'

'Surely the first thing is working out how we're going to gain access without being detected?' Fraser spoke up. Plunket shot the lieutenant a glance.

'There's no point in making it inside if there's nowhere to take the shot,' he told him, shifting his attention back to the larger map of Zaragoza. 'How wide is the river, and is there anywhere that might be suitable on the opposite bank? Does Dubertrand ever go down to the dock?'

'Perhaps, but only when a new shipment is ready to be transported. It's moved along the covered way. Besides, there is an outwork on the northern bank, protecting the approach. The river is about a hundred yards wide.'

'It's going to have to be from inside,' Mackintosh commented, eyes on the map of the fort's interior. 'Too many variables elsewhere.'

'There's enough of us to cover those variables,' Plunket said.

'If you trust anyone but yourself to take the shot.' Jones grinned.

'I don't think the duke or his pet spymaster cares who kills the chemist, only that he dies,' Plunket pointed out, before speaking to El Cruz again. 'You said if anyone is sick, they're removed from the workforce. If they recover, are they allowed back in?'

'No,' El Cruz said. 'But sometimes they bring in new people from the town to bolster numbers. After Zaragoza was sacked, many are just happy to take regular food and lodgings, even if it means labouring for the invader.'

Maria turned aside and spat on the straw-covered floor.

'I don't think I could pass as a Spanish labourer,' Fraser said. The riflemen laughed and Plunket shook his head.

'You won't need to. Once we reach Zaragoza, you'll be staying as far out of harm's way as possible.'

Fraser frowned and began to argue, but Plunket ignored him.

'We'll divide our strength to improve our chances,' he said. 'One posted on the north bank, as near as can be to the wharf without risking detection, the others inside the fort. If we can't use the workforce as cover, perhaps we can infiltrate on the barges themselves. When is the next shipment expected?'

'Difficult to say,' El Cruz admitted. 'We'll know more once we've made contact with the town and those inside the fort.'

'It could take weeks before the right opportunity presents itself,' Plunket cautioned. 'We'll need to be patient. That includes all of you.'

He made a point of looking at Carlos and Maria, on either side of El Cruz. Their father held his hand up before they could make any reply.

'Do not concern yourself with those under my command, *saltamontes*,' he said. 'They will not be found wanting.'

'We'll speak again when we have more current intelligence,' Plunket suggested.

After they had left the barn, Plunket drew Mackintosh to one side.

'Have you noticed any arguments between the Spaniards since we joined them?' he asked the Scot. 'Anything I might not have spotted?'

'What do you mean?' Mackintosh asked.

'The first night, while I was patrolling, I heard El Cruz's boy talking to a woman. I think it might have been the daughter, Maria. They'd left the camp. They didn't know I was there.'

'And you don't know what was said between them?'

'No, but it wasn't particularly fraternal-sounding. I think they could be hiding something from El Cruz.'

'Which probably isn't good news for any of us,' Mackintosh said. 'But if we don't know what they were saying, we can't exactly go to El Cruz about it. You know what the Spanish think of you. We start poking ourselves into their affairs, best case is they abandon us. And worst case, they try and slit our throats in the middle of the night...'

Plunket had already considered such possibilities. He couldn't imagine El Cruz turning on them, even given the antagonism he had initially displayed. He didn't know about the rest of the partisans though. Most seemed to follow El Cruz's orders without question, but they were a lean, hungry-looking lot, and Plunket suspected a few considered him almost as much of an enemy as the French.

'Best we can do for now is keep a sharp eye,' Plunket said.

'Always do,' Mackintosh responded. 'At least we're almost at Zaragoza.'

THEY PICKED UP signs of the French the next day.

The expedition passed by a towering old red-bricked citadel perched upon a cliffside, the medieval Castillo de Peracense. The road beyond it was marked by numerous fresh hoofprints, churned up by the passage of dozens of riders. Several partisans went ahead and spoke to the villagers in the next hamlet, who confirmed a large patrol of French dragoons had ridden through that morning.

They were deep in enemy territory now, and a single mistake could be fatal.

El Cruz directed the band through lesser-known herder's tracks and small valleys, leaving the beaten path altogether at times to cross bare fields or pick their way through woodland. The pace of the ride slowed, but Plunket made no complaint. They had no choice other than to trust the guerillas to lead them on.

They saw a French patrol late that evening, scouring the next valley along. El Cruz adjusted their course east, and they rode through the night, only snatching a few hours of sleep by the side of the path.

The journey was starting to take its toll on the British. Plunket had grown up around horses on the estate his father had worked as a gamekeeper, though this was far more riding than he was accustomed to. That was doubly so for the other three riflemen, all of whom were rudimentary equestrians at best. They were growing increasingly fatigued, and tempers were beginning to fray at the edges.

The day before they were due to reach Zaragoza, they rode through a valley overlooked on one side by a tall cross, erected on its rightmost summit. Plunket had seen such monuments in Iberia before – they reminded him of the old, mossy crucifixes and standing stones in Ireland, the ones his father had almost convinced him had been built by God-fearing giants in ages past.

There was a cart in the valley, off to the side of the track, close to a small stream that was babbling down through slope's rocks. It had thrown a wheel, and two peasants were working to repair it. The horses, two of them, had been unhitched and were grazing near the brook.

'We should keep riding,' Plunket called out to El Cruz as they went. 'This is a bad place to stop.'

'Agreed,' El Cruz called back. '*Vamos!*'

The column carried on as El Cruz peeled off to join Carlos, who appeared to be interrogating the two peasants closely. Plunket twisted in his saddle to look back at them. They had spoken to plenty of people throughout the journey so far – almost every Spaniard was willing to assist the guerrillas with information – but the convenience of these ones struck Plunket as odd.

His eyes strayed again to the horses grazing at the foot of the slope. They both had nagged tails, the hair cropped back almost to the bone.

He had rarely seen such a practice among the horses of Spanish peasants, but it was commonplace in both the British and French armies.

Those two weren't carthorses. They were cavalry mounts.

Plunket turned to Fraser, who was riding on his immediate left.

'It's a trap,' he shouted over the thunder of hooves. 'Tell them it's a trap!'

Too late. There was a cracking sound, and suddenly the whole valley was echoing with gunfire.

Chapter Nine

South of Zaragoza, North-Eastern Spain,
October 23rd, 1809

PLUNKET SAWED ON the reins as the partisan riding in front of him did likewise, his horse shying. He heard bullets whip by. Fraser had also come to a sudden stop next to him.

'We need to keep going,' he shouted at the lieutenant. 'Tell them we need to keep going!'

Fraser tried to do so, but it was useless. They were under fire from the left-hand slope ahead and the right-hand slope behind, green-coated figures darting between the rocks along the valley sides. French dragoons; dismounted and lying in wait.

They had known they were coming.

A bullet struck the horse of the partisan in front of Plunket and the beast went down, throwing its rider. They were penned in on the track, easy targets while mounted.

'Damn it,' Plunket spat, and kicked his heels from the stirrups, dropping down to the ground. Smith, Mackintosh and Jones were dismounting as well, coming to the same realisation that he had – riflemen didn't fight from horseback.

El Cruz's partisans were starting to scatter, some making for the head of the valley, running the gauntlet of carbine shots, while several others tried to charge the slopes. They were easily cut down, a dozen or more dragoons focusing their fire on them. A few others were doing as the riflemen were, dismounting and darting for the nearest rocks before starting to return fire.

'Hit the nearest, and push up the slope,' Plunket shouted at Jones, Smith and Mackintosh, pointing towards the right side of the valley ahead, where the gun smoke betrayed the fact that there were fewer dragoons. Not wanting to risk a crossfire hitting their own men, the French had deployed in such a way that the slope opposite their two concentrations was almost unoccupied, meaning that while the left side in front of the column was ablaze with carbine fire, the right side was almost clear.

Another bullet slapped past. Plunket heard a shout just to his left, and was amazed to see Fraser, still mounted, struggling with his horse. His bright scarlet coat made him the easiest target in the valley.

'Off the horse, Fraser, damn it,' Plunket shouted, lunging forward to grab the bridle of the officer's mount. Fraser seemed to have frozen again, the way Plunket had seen him seize up while being ridden down by a dragoon just north of the Guadiana.

In the end, the lieutenant didn't get a chance to dismount. His horse was hit, twice, shrieking with pain and bolting. Fraser was thrown and came down hard just before the brook.

Plunket scrambled to his side as he tried to get up, dragging him down again, into the meagre cover of a few rocks. The youth had lost his hat and looked dazed.

'Stick with me and Mackintosh, and keep your damned big head down,' Plunket snapped at him, as Mackintosh darted across the path to join them.

'Nearest is a hundred yards up, on your right,' the rifleman said, indicating a stretch of the slope higher up.

'Take him,' Plunket instructed, while starting to load.

Mackintosh steadied his Baker rifle on one of the rocks, then fired. Plunket didn't see if he hit his mark – he was too busy priming. When he was finished, he waited for Mackintosh, picking his target as he did so and lining up his sights.

'Loaded,' the Scotsman declared.

Plunket fired. Smoke shrouded his view, but he was moving anyway, darting through it and up the slope to the next set of rocks. He hit the dirt behind them, heart racing, hearing a flurry of cracking sounds as return fire peppered his newfound cover.

He began to reload.

Smith and Jones were doing the same a little further along, putting into practice the method of fighting that the British Army had first learned in North America over half a century previously – skirmishing in pairs, making use of cover, one man loading while the other fired and manoeuvred. It was the form of combat taught at the light infantry training school at Shorncliffe, and it was how the green-jacketed riflemen made war on their enemies.

'Loaded,' Plunket barked back to Mackintosh, not looking at him, his eyes instead scanning the slope for the next nearest threat. He heard Mackintosh's discharge and saw a dragoon reel back a second after appearing from behind the trunk of a withered old tree clinging to the slope, his carbine unfired.

A pounding of feet, and Mackintosh dropped in next to him. Plunket was glad to see Fraser was with him – the youth seemed to have recovered some of his wits and had drawn his sword, his expression wide-eyed and tense with fear and excitement.

Bullets buzzed and whistled overhead, like angry insects. The French were firing high, a common mistake. Though they carried carbines, most dragoons were more accustomed to acting as sword-wielding cavalrymen, rather than fighting in their old role as mounted infantry.

'Last shot was good,' Plunket told Mackintosh while he hunted for his next target, letting the other rifleman reload before firing.

He moved again, feet splashing in the brook, nearly slipping but managing to keep his balance. The cross was above them, standing proud at the valley's summit, silhouetted by the lowering sun. It hadn't been occupied by the dragoons, as it would have left their smoothbore carbines out of range of the valley floor. That was a blessing Plunket intended to make the most of.

He dropped in behind another scrabbly tree and reached for more powder and ball. It was difficult work, maintaining such a rate of fire with patched bullets, and he knew that he'd have another dozen or so shots before the barrel began to foul up with sticky gunpowder residue, clogging the barrel grooves and making it more and more difficult to ram charge. Once it got too choked, he'd be defenceless, besides the long sword bayonet hanging at his hip.

He took stock as he reloaded. The valley was still in chaos, but the nearest partisans had seen the weakness the riflemen were seeking to exploit and were joining them in their push on that side, their own style of irregular warfare not dissimilar from the way the British were fighting. If they kept advancing, they'd make the crest, and in doing so hopefully punch through the ambush. After that, it would be a matter of praying for the onset of night. Plunket knew how bleak the odds were of surviving on foot while being pursued across the Spanish countryside in daylight once the dragoons remounted.

Mackintosh and Fraser caught up, and Plunket put a ball through another dragoon who unwisely exposed himself to take a shot. He glanced left down the slope as he began to reload again, checking that Smith and Jones were making their own progress. That part of the valley was rockier, so they had dropped a little behind.

Plunket was just priming, about to tell Mackintosh to make his next run, when the Scotsman spoke.

'You feel that?'

Plunket paused and picked up what the other rifleman had already felt. There was a tremor running through the rocky soil underfoot, and with it came a rising rumble, echoing along the valley. It was a sound Plunket recognised all too well.

'Hooves,' he said grimly.

The source of the thunder came into view. A column of French cavalry swept from the head of the valley, surging along the track. These were not the green-coated dragoons, but a breed of horsemen even more feared and hated by British light infantrymen – lancers. They wore tall, square hats called *czapka* and carried their namesake weapon, a ten-foot pole tipped with a wicked steel spike, above a streaming red-and-white pennant. Plunket had seen them in action during the retreat to Corunna and had heard plenty of stories about how the Polish lancers in service to Napoleon had routed Spanish forces elsewhere in Iberia.

The lances made spearing fleeing infantry akin to child's play. The sight of them caused a thrill of fear sharp enough to cut through the cold clarity that Plunket always found settled over him during combat.

'Up the slope,' he shouted to the British and any Spaniards who were listening, pointing towards the cross on the summit above them. 'Move!'

The valley sides were steep and rocky, especially at the top – no place for cavalry. That was their only hope now.

The lancers came on with a whooping yell, first striking the small number of mounted partisans who had successfully run the gauntlet of dragoon fire. They were ridden down with ease. The lancers then spread out across the valley bottom, beginning to hunt the partisans who had scattered individually or in small groups.

'Come on,' Plunket shouted furiously towards the nearest Spaniards, as well as Jones and Smith. The two riflemen were still lower down the slope. Smith fired while Jones ran, toppling one of the lancers, before the Englishman took to his heels as well, scrambling over the rocks.

Plunket finished reloading, snapping at Mackintosh and Fraser to keep going. Then he crouched by the tree again and used one of the branches as a rest. A trio of lancers were in pursuit, taking to the foot of the slope, the pennants near the tips of their long weapons fluttering and snapping.

Plunket fired, rifle butt kicking his shoulder, the branches of the old tree rattling around him. One of the horses went down, lance snapping under its weight as the rider went with it.

Jones fired and Smith ran. More lancers had spotted the greenjackets, a whoop going up as they recognised British riflemen among the Spanish guerrillas.

'Come on,' Plunket shouted at his men.

Mackintosh, stopping higher up, fired, but the ball went wide. One of the lancers had turned away to ride down a nearby partisan who had fired at him and missed. The other spurred on relentlessly after the riflemen, horse leaping and bounding up the increasingly steep, craggy slope.

Jones and Smith weren't going to make it. Plunket began to reload feverishly, not bothering with the patch this time, sacrificing accuracy for speed.

'Corporal, get back,' he heard Fraser shouting at him from higher up the slope, but he ignored the lieutenant. He lifted his rifle back to the branch, but he was too late.

Smith had tripped and fallen. As he scrambled up, the lancer bore down on him from behind. The wicked weapon rammed forward, slicing through Smith's knapsack and piercing his spine. The rifleman gave a terrible shriek.

Plunket and Mackintosh fired at the same time. The lancer's horse tumbled – Plunket had no idea if one or both of them had hit it, but it didn't matter. He had already begun to scramble back downhill, towards Jones and Smith, heedless of the shouts of Mackintosh and Fraser, of the dragoon bullets still whipping by, or the next group of lancers kicking their mounts up towards them.

Jones had doubled back to Smith and was dispatching the lancer with his sword bayonet as Plunket reached them, the cavalryman trapped and helpless under his dead mount. Plunket knelt beside Smith, turning him onto his side as gently as possible, but it was immediately clear the rifleman was dead. His eyes were glassy, and blood was drooling thick and dark from his slack mouth.

Plunket felt a surge of bitter anger. He knew he couldn't let it get the better of him, or they'd all end up the same way. He picked up Smith's rifle and stood, shouting to Jones.

'Get up the damn slope! Now!'

They set off at a run, Plunket's legs starting to burn and his lungs to ache as he pushed himself on. A pair of Spaniards had made it up out of the valley as well and were nearly at the crest. Mackintosh fired again over their heads, while Fraser was gesturing desperately with his sword. Plunket could hear the gallows drumbeat of hooves behind him but didn't dare snatch a glance back.

The cross was just above them now, backlit by the setting sun, burning itself into his eyes as he looked up. He reached for it as though he was reaching for salvation, expecting at the same time to feel the agony of a piercing blow, fearing that he would be forced to scream that terrible scream Smith had made.

The Spaniards had made it to the crest with Fraser and Mackintosh. One of them fired his musket. Then Plunket was scrabbling over the rocks directly beneath the cross, on flat ground, turning at bay, panting, snarling.

Five lancers had hounded them almost to the base of the cross, but they were struggling to urge their mounts up the last few yards, which were almost sheer. The incline was less severe to the left, and they began to turn their horses in that direction.

The second Spaniard fired and brought one down. Barely able to breathe, Plunket reloaded as fast as he could.

Now, suddenly, the lancers were at a disadvantage. Mackintosh, Jones then Plunket all fired into them at close range, knocking two from their saddles and dropping another horse. The last rider wheeled away, galloping precipitously back down the slope.

The riflemen and the Spaniards reloaded, and Plunket passed Fraser Smith's rifle as well as a few of cartridges from his main pouch.

'Any of the bastards ride close, shoot them,' he ordered the little band of survivors.

Several more lancers tried their luck, but the gunfire combined with the steepness of the final ascent dissuaded them from pressing the attack. The partisans still on the valley floor and lower slopes were far easier targets, and as darkness began to fall and the shadows pooled beneath, Plunket watched the French complete the destruction of El Cruz's guerrillas.

'We need to get moving,' he said, knowing that the safety of the summit was illusory – once more attention turned their way, they would quickly be surrounded and cut down, if not by the lancers, then by the dismounted dragoons.

'Look there,' Fraser cried out, taking one hand from his newly acquired rifle to point along the slope.

Plunket saw what he had spotted. A knot of partisan riders had almost made it away from the massacre. One was skewered off his horse by a pursuing lancer, but three more managed to gain the crest further along, before turning towards the summit and its cross.

Plunket didn't need to issue orders. A few more rifle shots warded off further pursuit.

The riders reached the cross, and Plunket found he recognised two – El Cruz's son and daughter. Carlos had apparently lost his musket at some point as well as his hat and was white-faced and visibly trembling. Maria was the opposite, flushed with a ferocious anger. She carried a sabre, and its wicked edge was red.

She spat something vehement in Spanish towards the riflemen and gestured with the blade down into the valley.

'She… wants to know why you aren't fighting,' Fraser suggested.

'Tell her if she wants to die, she's welcome to go back the way she came,' Plunket said. 'And then ask her where El Cruz is.'

'She says her father was one of the first to die,' Fraser said after a shot, sharp exchange. 'A musket ball… tore his throat.'

Plunket had feared as much.

'We need to get moving, before they come after us in force,' he told Fraser, who passed it on. 'We have to make the most of the coming darkness. Get as close to Zaragoza as possible.'

He expected disagreement at best, and at worst for the three Spanish riders to simply gallop off. Instead, Maria and Carlos had a brief conversation, before Carlos spoke in broken English.

'Will not be able to make Zaragoza before dawn, not on foot,' he said. 'Maybe by tomorrow night.'

'Either way, we're not staying here,' Plunket said. He pointed down the opposite side of the crest, towards the neighbouring valley, and the forest visible beyond. 'Right now what matters is getting away from here.'

The partisans agreed. Plunket had Mackintosh take the lead while he brought up the rear. He spared one more glance down into the valley of death, searching for a glimpse of Smith's body, but twilight's shadows had crept up the slope now and turned everything below into a pool of darkness, shot through with the hint of hurrying figures and the occasional flash of discharges, as the last of El Cruz's band were hunted down.

It felt wrong to leave them, to leave Smith, but Plunket knew they didn't have a choice.

They hastened across into the next valley, leaving death and desolation in their wake.

Chapter Ten

South of Zaragoza, North-Eastern Spain,
October 24th, 1809

IT WAS A sleepless, nerve-ridden night. They made the forest before dark but quickly lost their bearing and could make no further progress without running the risk of going in circles. Plunket ordered them to take shelter in a small dell they stumbled across, and they spent the remaining hours in fretful worry, weapons primed, straining for signs that they had been discovered.

The French were hunting them. They heard movement not long before the dawn, as patrols scoured the woodland. At one point, Carlos and Maria got into a hissing argument, and Plunket was on the cusp of snapping at them to shut up when, to his surprise, Fraser whispered something sharply in Spanish that seemed to run along the same lines.

Plunket found himself remembering their last nighttime argument. What had they been saying, away from their fellow partisans, and their father? Had they known what would be lying in wait for them before they reached Zaragoza?

Later, he realised Carlos was weeping bitterly in the dark, presumably over the loss of his father. Plunket understood the weight of emotion but kept it in check. There would be a time for anger and regret, but right now those feelings would do none of them any good.

When the dawn began to show its slender grey fingers through the foliage, they moved. Beyond the forest's edge the partisans discovered a farmhouse that one of them said he recognised. It was long-abandoned, stripped bare months ago by French marauders, but it allowed them to get their bearings.

They turned north, avoiding main roads and well-used tracks. Hoof prints betrayed the passage of large numbers of horsemen in the area, but they saw no other signs of the enemy until midday, when a plume of smoke indicated a burning homestead.

They avoided it, and later took shelter in another copse of trees, when a party of French dragoons came into sight along the crest of a nearby hillock.

It was slow going on foot, and hunger and exhaustion had started to gnaw at them. Not long after midday, one of the partisans spoke up.

'He says he's leaving,' Fraser translated. 'That he's going to find food, and he'll rejoin us in Zaragoza.'

Plunket's rifle was loaded, and he took it from his shoulder, thumb curled around the cock, before speaking.

'Tell him he's not going anywhere,' he ordered Fraser, while looking the partisan dead in the eyes. The entire group had come to a halt.

'If he wants to leave, we let him,' Carlos said, frowning at Plunket. 'He is a good man. He will rejoin us. If it were not for my sister, I would go with him.'

'The French knew we were coming,' Plunket told Carlos. 'That entire ambush was orchestrated. That means someone told them where we'd be, and when. And somehow, I don't think it was Lieutenant Fraser, or any of my riflemen.'

'You are calling us traitors?' Carlos snapped. 'Do you know how many of us were killed yesterday? My own father—'

'Someone talked,' Plunket said. 'And right now, I can't risk the fact it might have been him.'

He nodded at the partisan who had suggested leaving, before going on.

'If he's on the side of the French, he'll ride to their garrison in Zaragoza and make sure they finish what he started yesterday. So he stays. You all stay, and we make contact with the rest of your friends in Zaragoza together. And if any of you try to ride off, I, or Rifleman Jones or Rifleman Mackintosh, will shoot you.'

Carlos looked unhappy, but after a short conversation the Spaniard who had suggested leaving shrugged his shoulders and began to walk his horse along the pathway they had been taking. The group resumed its journey, undivided, though Plunket kept his rifle cradled in his arms, the flint at half cock.

Not long after they had started to walk again, Fraser fell in beside Plunket.

'We're not turning back?' the young lieutenant muttered. Plunket glanced at him.

'Why would we?'

'There's almost none of us left. And you said it yourself, the French know we're coming.'

'The Spaniards were only supposed to get us into Fort Josephine, and they can still do that,' Plunket pointed out. 'It's up to one of the riflemen to make the kill, and there are still three of us. It only takes a single shot.'

'But the odds,' Fraser began to say, before trailing off, clearly not wanting to admit to any further concerns.

'You're not a greenjacket, so I won't think any worse of you,' Plunket told the young man. 'But the Rifles are the first into the action, and the last out of it. And this battle isn't over yet.'

THAT AFTERNOON THEY stopped in a tavern where the owner gave them bread and cheese and wine, and told them he had heard of French troops criss-crossing the countryside, but had not seen any for himself. He permitted them to sleep for a few hours in the tavern's stables.

Plunket knew it was a risk but knew too that they couldn't run indefinitely without food or sleep. He took the first watch, and had planned on taking it all until, after an hour, Mackintosh appeared and demanded he get some rest.

That had always been the way. Plunket, Mackintosh and Smith had been serving together since meeting at the 1805 recruitment intake at Shorncliffe barracks, while Jones had joined them in the Peninsular. Over the past four years they had endured enough hardship for decades of military service – first the brutalities of the Buenos Aires expedition, to campaigning in Portugal under Wellesley, now the Duke of Wellington. Worst of all had been the retreat to Corunna, conducted through the rough Galician hill country in the depths of winter, hounded every step of the way by the French.

At times, Plunket thought he couldn't go on, but the others had always been there for him, just as he had been there for them. They had shared every scrap of rations they had, and by some miracle that ragged, skeletal army had held itself together long enough not only to reach the coast, but to turn at bay and savage their French pursuers in pitched battle before boarding the Royal Navy's ships.

The army had recovered, and returned, and had won another victory at Talavera that summer, though it hardly seemed to have made a difference – the French forces in Iberia appeared to be numberless, as they were all over Europe, their emperor's rule now barely challenged from Madrid to Warsaw. Plunket had no doubt that, if properly supplied, they would overrun Wellington and what parts of Spain remained unconquered, followed by Portugal.

After that, Napoleon's eagles would be masters of the greater part of Europe.

So Plunket would keep going, despite the death of Smith and most of the partisans. He knew turning back now would be pointless anyway – he doubted they would make it across Spain to Wellington's army alone. Their only choice was to try and reach Zaragoza and hope they could fashion a new scheme that would get the French chemist in their sights.

The little group set out again after darkness. Fraser and the one Spaniard without a horse mounted up behind those who did, while the trio of riflemen moved at the quick step used by the 95th, walking for three paces, then trotting for three, and alternating between the two. Plunket knew the best thing now would be to force himself through his own tiredness, rather than prolong the struggle by permitting them all to slow down.

They reached the outskirts of the town before the dawn. It had been the scene of ferocious fighting at the start of the year, a fact that became rapidly apparent before they had even entered the town proper. They stopped at a villa by the road, its white walls scarred and pockmarked by musket balls, its lower windows boarded up. The outbuildings were just blackened ruins.

A serving maid answered the door, holding a candle aloft and peering at the bedraggled band on the doorstep. She retreated briefly, before returning and ushering them inside while another servant took the horses.

'This is the home of a merchant my father knows,' Carlos said. 'He and his family fled before the French came, but he permits us to stay when we need to. We are safe here.'

After what had happened, Plunket didn't know how true that statement was, but he understood they had no choice other than to hope Carlos was correct, for now.

They slept away what remained of the night in the kitchen and cellar, their rifles close at hand.

The next morning, over a breakfast of bread and cold meats, Plunket spoke with Carlos and Maria, with Fraser and the other riflemen in attendance.

'The plan still stands,' he told them. 'My men and I need to get into Fort Josephine.'

'It is madness to try now,' Carlos complained. 'They will know we are coming!'

'What they know, is that a force of partisans was practically wiped out over a day's ride south of here,' Plunket said. 'What do you think whoever was in charge of that ambush will emphasise? That half a dozen of the enemy escaped and are currently at large, or that the enemy were all-but destroyed, with a few survivors scattered through the countryside? If they identified the body of your father, they'll report that the leader of the partisans has been killed as well. As far as the commander of the garrison here will be concerned, what threat we posed is now gone. And that gives us a chance.'

Maria said something which caused a flash of annoyance to cross Carlos's face.

'She wants to fight,' Fraser told Plunket simply.

'Ask her how many partisans they have among the workforce inside the factory,' Plunket said.

'Not many,' Fraser said after listening to her reply. 'But the workers can be roused to help if need be. They have managed to get some weapons inside Fort Josephine, and they could cause havoc with the garrison if need be.'

'Can she get word to the workforce? Prepare them for what is to come?'

'Apparently, yes. She says she can go herself.'

Carlos snapped something at his sister.

'He says she should not be risking her life for this Englishman,' Fraser told Plunket while looking darkly at the Spaniard. 'He says we are doomed, and that the whole plan was foolish from the beginning. We cannot stop the factory's production.'

'We're not trying to stop production, not directly,' Plunket said to Carlos. 'Killing Dubertrand will do that for us.'

'If you incite a riot in the factory, many innocents will be killed,' Carlos complained.

'You were the ones who requested our aid,' Fraser said before Plunket could respond. 'We are risking everything to deal a blow to Bonaparte, to liberate your country.'

'The English and liberty are rarely on the same side,' Carlos said.

Maria, clearly doing her best to follow the conversation, spoke again.

'She wants to know if you will let her reach out to the partisans in the town, and then the fort,' he said. 'She is proposing travelling into Fort Josephine herself, as soon as possible.'

Plunket considered the possibility. It was a risk. He thought about the ambush, about the argument he had heard Carlos having on that first night, with a woman he was now sure was Maria. Had they known? But he could think of no way they could get into Fort Josephine and have any hope of eliminating Dubertrand without the help of the Spanish.

'You and your brother spoke together on the first night after my men and I joined you,' Plunket said to Maria, looking at the young woman as Fraser translated. 'You argued, and you thought you did it out of earshot. What did you say to each other?'

Maria failed to mask her surprise. She glanced furtively at her brother, whose expression grew even angrier than before.

'That is none of your concern, skulking grasshopper!'

'I think it might be. I think one of you knew what was waiting for us in that valley, and you were trying to convince the other not to go. Did you try to tell your father as well, or did you think he would be too stubborn, too dedicated to his cause?'

Carlos grew so angry he began snapping at Plunket in Spanish, but Maria started to speak as well, her voice rising above his. Fraser translated hastily.

'She says they argued, yes, but there was never any talk of treachery, or a trap. Carlos said the English had not provided enough aid. He wanted to abandon the plan and wanted her help in convincing their father.'

'Is that because you had already sent word ahead, to warn the French?' Plunket demanded of Carlos. 'But you couldn't admit as much to your sister and father, because you knew they would never assist the invader. So you were looking for an excuse to convince them not to ride into that death trap.'

'Go to hell, Englishman,' Carlos snarled, before turning and storming out. Maria shouted something after him, but he ignored it.

'Go after him,' Plunket growled to Mackintosh and Jones. 'Make sure he doesn't leave.'

The two greenjackets stalked out after the Spaniard, leaving Plunket with Maria and Fraser. Plunket looked at her for a while, and she returned his gaze defiantly.

'I do not trust your brother,' Plunket told her, via Fraser. 'But I also know I won't be able to get inside that fort without your help. So, tell me, should I let you ride into town?'

'She says you must forgive her brother, that he has an academic mind. He is not made for this sort of thing.'

'But she is?' Plunket asked.

'When the French came to Zaragoza, they burned the place she had just started to call home and abused and murdered her sisters. The nuns, I think she means. She says she does not care if you think she is a traitor or not. She knows in her own mind, that she would rather slit her own throat, than ever accept the occupation of her country at the hands of the Bonapartists.'

Plunket believed her.

'Ask if she's ready to go into the fort,' he said. Fraser smiled sheepishly.

'I don't think we need to ask her that. She's ready.'

Chapter Eleven

Zaragoza, North-Eastern Spain,
October 26th, 1809

MARIA ENTERED ZARAGOZA proper and returned that evening with several partisans who had remained in the town. Plunket produced Simpson's maps, and they again discussed possibilities and potential problems.

To his surprise, Carlos had sought him out earlier that afternoon and made a halting apology.

'I grieve for my father, *señor*,' he admitted. 'My anger, it comes from frustration. Your Duke Wellington has not provided enough men to aid us. I knew that from the beginning. I wish I could have convinced my father to turn back, before it was too late.'

'It isn't over yet,' Plunket assured him.

Maria delivered her report. The barges, Plunket learned, were on their way. The network of informants that kept news flowing about French movements throughout Spain had got word that a flotilla of flat-bottomed boats were passing along the Ebro and were expected to reach Zaragoza in a little over two days. The partisans identified the place the barges were likely to spend the night, at a smaller settlement that straddled the river further to the north-west.

'Can we make that place before they leave?' Plunket asked, running through the possibilities in his head.

According to the partisans, they could. Plunket outlined his plan.

'It is madness,' Carlos said, his truce with Plunket seemingly already abandoned.

'If you have a better idea for reaching Dubertrand, suggest it,' Plunket said, in no mood to indulge the Spaniard's reluctance any longer. 'If you're afraid, then don't come. We'll have no use for you. Your sister can take your place.'

The comment stung Carlos into acceptance. That night, they rode west.

THE PLAN WAS audacious, but Plunket told himself he'd beaten worse odds.

The partisans made contact with a ferryman west of Zaragoza and convinced him to take them upriver. The night suited their purposes well, the moon shrouded by thick cloud. It was cold, but the servants at the merchant's house had furnished the riflemen with a few old cloaks, for which they were thankful.

They rowed against the current, Plunket soon finding his arms and shoulders beginning to ache with the effort. Mackintosh, Jones and Fraser were all present, as was Carlos and one other partisan from Zaragoza: Antonio, apparently a distant cousin of the El Cruz family. Maria had left earlier in an attempt to rejoin the workforce within the fort – it would be far easier for her to slip inside, compared to the four British soldiers, especially since Plunket refused to allow them to remove their uniforms. It was the only insurance they had against execution if they were taken, and while Plunket wouldn't admit it out loud, capture seemed like a certainty. He was certain Mackintosh and Jones knew that, and that Fraser was coming to accept it. He also had no doubt that both Simpson and Robertson had known they wouldn't be returning to the army encamped on the Guadiana.

Damn them all to hell, Plunket thought. He would do his duty regardless. All he needed was one shot.

* * *

As Plunket had hoped, there was no sign of any guards on the barges themselves – they had not yet taken on the cargo they were going to Fort Josephine to collect, and so they lay empty as their crews ate and drank in the tavern close to the wharf.

They slid up alongside the foremost boat, trying to go as silently as possible. The transports were sleek craft, with short masts to accommodate a jib and mainstay sail. They reminded Plunket of the wine boats he had seen on the Duro, during the battle of Porto earlier that year.

They stood on their oars, and Antonio was able to reach out and snatch the bow. Jones and then Plunket did likewise, helping drag the small ferryboat alongside while Antonio lashed a rope between the two transports, temporarily anchoring them.

They transferred over, the movements clumsy and loud in the dark, the boats creaking and knocking up against one another. At one point the tavern door opened, emitting a surge of chatter and laughter from within, as well as the sound of a violin. Light spilled out across the wharf, and the little expedition froze, half-in, half-out, as a Spaniard wandered out. Drunk, he staggered slightly and turned to piss up against the tavern wall before returning inside to a chorus of shouts and jeers, oblivious to what was unfolding mere feet away.

Plunket was the last to cross, slinging his rifle and tossing his shako over ahead of him. That left only the ferryman, who unlashed the rope once they were across. He would drift back east with the current, home by the dawn.

'Oars?' Plunket asked softly as he settled himself in their new transport.

'Stowed,' Mackintosh confirmed, reaching down to pat one of the wooden beams in the dark. Plunket peered at where he found himself, relieved to discover, as he had hoped, that the bilge was beneath a layer of spare canvas sails. That would be where the gunpowder barrels would be secured for the return trip from Fort Josephine but, for now, the space was empty and, just as importantly, covered.

The party concealed themselves there, between the benches and their stowed oars. Plunket settled in on the hard, wet bottom boards, and forced himself to put his mind elsewhere, to wait and not let the burden of anticipation drag him down and flood his mind with doubts.

Dawn seemed to take a long time to come. When it did, the crewmen took even longer to reassemble, their schedule apparently unhurried. Plunket listened as they boarded, the boat creaking. There was coughing, spitting, muttering; brief, low laughter. He heard ropes clapping against the mast and the whoosh of the small sails being unfurled and watched in breathless tension as shoes and lower legs passed him by, the crewmen manoeuvring around the canvas covering to seat themselves along the thwarts. The oars were picked up, and after a while a voice began to call out the strokes, getting the rowers into a rhythm.

The barge began to move, gliding along the river. Plunket exchanged a glance with Jones and Mackintosh, their expressions barely discernible in the shadows beneath the canvas. He shook his head.

Let them row, for now.

He did his best to keep a mental count of the time since the crews returned. The ferryman had told him roughly how long it would take to row downriver and reach Zaragoza. After about half an hour, he tapped the riflemen and Antonio on the shoulder, the prearranged signal.

Antonio cocked the pistol he was carrying, and slid partly out from under the canvas, up at the barge's stern.

There, the master of the little crew started, staring down at him.

The partisan spoke, in a low voice, presumably telling the surprised man not to cry out.

Following Antonio's instructions, the boat master explained to his men that there were partisans onboard, and that they were not to react or stop rowing. Plunket eased back part of the canvas, pointing his rifle at the oarsman seated just above him without rising up into view beyond the boat's gunwales. The man just gaped at him in shock, so Plunket tapped his weapon's muzzle lightly against the man's ankle, and he hastily resumed his rowing.

Antonio slipped up to sit alongside the boat master, keeping his pistol low.

'You've told them they won't be harmed if they just keep rowing for the fort?' Plunket asked Carlos, who had stayed down. He shot a glance up at the other partisan, then nodded.

THE BARGE CREW rediscovered their rhythm. The riflemen and Fraser stayed down in the bilge, their weapons cocked and covering the oarsmen, so close the muzzles were nearly pressed against them. Plunket had Carlos stay down for the most part as well, not wanting to risk someone on one of the barges further back noticing that there seemed to be too many crewmen onboard the lead transport.

The current and a fair wind helped carry the boats downriver more swiftly than the ferryman had brought them up it. A little after midday, Antonio passed a message on to Fraser, who translated to Plunket.

'He says the fort is in sight. We will be at the wharf in half an hour.'

Plunket resisted the urge to rise and peer over the gunwales. The moment of greatest danger was approaching, and every possible risk had to be minimised.

'Tell him to keep describing what's happening, but not too loud,' Plunket told Fraser.

The partisan talked about the approach, and Plunket visualised the squat, angular dirt walls of the fort, the foreboding, dark barrels of cannons jutting from embrasures, the snatched glimpses of blue-coated French soldiers patrolling the bastions, the tricolour fluttering above the gatehouse. Beyond it all, there were structures that stood proud of the defences, including the factory itself, with its four great brick chimneys, churning out smoke.

Plunket smelled the place before he saw it, that familiar, sulphuric stink of gunpowder catching in the back of his throat, so pungent he felt as though he could taste it. He caught sight of the smoke next: a morose, dirty cloud hanging heavy in the sky ahead, fed by those four pillars of industry.

He checked his rifle and nodded to the others, no words required.

Make ready.

Fraser translated Antonio's description of the wharf as they drew towards it – it consisted of a trio of timber jetties, jutting out into the river. They protruded from a gap in the sections of the wall overlooking the Ebro, flanked by looming bastions and more artillery.

There were workers on the jetties, and stacks of barrels, the latest batch of gunpowder produced by the Fort Josephine factory. That was a relief, Plunket thought. If there had been any perceived danger from the river, the French presumably wouldn't have brought the precious, volatile barrels out.

This time, the enemy didn't know they were coming.

'Slow us down, and bring us to the furthest jetty,' Plunket instructed Antonio via Fraser, who issued a series of instructions to the boat master. The sails were furled and the barge brought in close to the riverbank, oars raised, running on the current.

'Shakos off, rifles under the cloaks, nice and easy,' Plunket instructed his men. They were tense, and he didn't blame them. There would be no room for manoeuvre, in any sense, and little opportunity to recover from any mistakes or unanticipated dangers.

When the time came, they would have to be fast.

Plunket heard voices calling out across the water in Spanish: the boat master and the workers on the dock exchanging greetings. He kept an eye on Antonio, still seated at the rear, pistol half hidden by the hem of his own cloak.

Lines were tossed and secured, and the timber of the barge creaked around Plunket as the boat was heaved in alongside the jetty.

Carlos had moved surreptitiously up into the boat's bow. Words were exchanged, Plunket still able to see little of what was going on. He looked at Fraser, his face shadowed by the canvas, trying to gauge from that pallid, nervous expression just what was being said.

Maria had promised that she would do her best to ensure workers friendly to the partisans were at the dock that afternoon. But what if she had failed? Or worse, what if she had betrayed them?

The boat shuddered as someone dropped down into it. Plunket found himself looking at a pair of dirty leather shoes and threadbare trousers.

More voices. Slowly, Plunket pulled his rifle's flint back to full cock.

The canvas was pulled away, and he angled the weapon up at the same time, poised to fire as a figure uncovered him.

Chapter Twelve

Fort Josephine, Zaragoza, North-Eastern Spain, October 27th, 1809

A YOUNG SPANIARD, his face and clothes smeared with soot, looked down at Plunket. He didn't seem surprised at having uncovered a green-jacketed Briton, pointing a rifle up at him. He grinned.

'*Buenos dias, saltamontes*,' he said.

Plunket relaxed fractionally and lowered his aim.

It seemed Maria had been as good as her word. All being well, the partisans posing as workers would help during the loading of the barges, smuggling the British inside at the same time.

'Easy now, lads,' Plunket quietly cautioned Fraser and the other riflemen. They stood cautiously, shakos off, cloaks on, doing their best to conceal their firearms. Plunket eased his rifle off full cock and looked around as he rose, breath baited.

The jetties were bustling with activity. Workers from the factory had started rolling barrels from a covered timber tunnel down short planks and onto the barges, the noise like a rumbling thunder. Men were shouting and gesturing back and forth, Plunket suspected in part to add to the chaos and further conceal the hidden cargo being brought into the fort.

There were blue-coated French infantry present, but there were only a few among the workers. Most were standing off beyond the wharf or on the neighbouring bastions, bored-looking as they watched the barges fill.

None appeared to have noticed the four new men among the busy workers.

Keeping their gaze low, the British made their way onto the jetty, joined by Carlos and Antonio.

Plunket took in the interior of the fort, now visible beyond the wharf's bustle. It matched the maps well enough – a handsome stone villa stood to the left of the central parade square, standing opposite the fire-scorched stone of an old, ruinous church. Beside the former place of worship were a series of timber structures that Plunket took to be stables, cookhouses, and the living quarters constructed for the factory's workforce.

The factory itself stood directly opposite the fort's riverside entrance, a megalith of red bricks and tall, narrow windows, crowned by four jagged pinnacles – the chimneys from which black, bitter smoke broiled, casting a pall over the entire fort. The covered walkway the barrels were being rolled down from led round the back of the villa to the factory's flank, forming a production line from the building to the river and then on, to Napoleon's armies throughout Spain.

The sight of such looming, rampant industry almost made Plunket hesitate. Then the defiance that had marked and marred so much of his life took hold, and he felt an upsurge of determination.

They were close. All that remained was to find Francois Dubertrand.

'Head along the jetty, nice and easy,' he instructed the others. There were labourers coming and going from the direction of both the factory and the workhouse buildings, which was just what they needed. They'd be able to join the flow of bodies and reach the church without drawing attention.

After that, it should simply be a case of securing its tower, and watching, and waiting.

They were almost off the back end of the wharf, passing beneath the bastions overlooking the river, when Carlos began to speak.

Plunket didn't understand what he was saying, but the meaning rapidly became apparent as his volume increased, until the Spaniard was shouting and gesturing towards the closest French soldiers.

Plunket realised he wasn't speaking Spanish, but French.

'What're you doing?' Jones snapped, grabbing Carlos's arm, but he snatched himself away and rounded on the rifleman, drawing a pistol.

Too late, Plunket understood his mistake.

It was Carlos who had told the French of the approach of El Cruz's expedition, and it was Carlos who was now, at the last moment, attempting to warn the garrison of the British soldiers in their midst.

'Run for the workhouses,' Plunket barked, throwing back his cloak and levelling his rifle at Carlos. 'Go, now!'

A number of the nearest Frenchmen had started to turn towards the commotion. Several began to call out. Muskets were being raised.

Carlos shot Jones.

THE RIFLEMEN FOLDED. Plunket let out a cry of rage and fired as well. The bullet took Carlos in the chest, splintering a rib and punching through a lung, killing the Spaniard.

The wharf descended into bedlam.

'Go,' Plunket roared. Mackintosh moved, but Plunket was forced to snatch Fraser's greatcoat and drag him along before the officer began to run of his own accord. He'd been staring at Jones, lying in the dust.

Plunket knew there was nothing they could do for him now.

One of the French soldiers fired, the musket ball thumping into the dirt and bouncing up just past Plunket's knee. He saw a French officer, gorget gleaming at his throat, waving both hands and smacking at the barrels of his nearest men, knocking the weapons down, presumably desperate to stop a stray shot or spark from hitting one of the powder barrels and blowing the entire fort to kingdom come.

That was the only advantage they had, and Plunket was determined to use it.

The British broke right, along the edge of the parade, trying to get round to the tangle of workhouses and outbuildings around the burned-out church. That was the only place that might offer even the possibility of evasion.

Workers were shouting and running back and forth, some of them starting to jostle and shove against the guards. Plunket didn't know if that was part of the plan, or just natural reactions amidst the chaos, but he was thankful for it.

Another gunshot rang out, presumably against orders. Plunket looked left as he ran, towards the villa, hunting for any sign of a man in civilian dress, for anyone who might be Dubertrand. If he could take the shot now, he would.

He knew it would likely be his only chance.

More gunshots, but this time they came from the windows of one of the wooden structures next to the church. He couldn't tell if it was the French firing at them, or more of Maria's partisan infiltrators. Carlos had betrayed them, but was his sister still loyal to her country, or the invaders?

Plunket decided that, at this point, it didn't matter. They made it into the shadow of the buildings on the right side of the parade, panting, Fraser shaking. His greatcoat was open, his red uniform bright in the shade thrown by the church looming over them.

'Keep going,' Plunket instructed. They turned towards the old, blackened structure, and had almost reached it just as a group of French soldiers burst from the alleyway between it and what Plunket took to be a stable block.

Both sides looked equally surprised, and there was almost no time to react. Plunket knocked aside one man's half-hearted attempt at a bayonet stab with his rifle's stock before reversing the shorter weapon and cracking it into the man's face, feeling bone break beneath its brass butt plate. Beside him, Fraser flung himself with a shout against another Frenchman, seemingly forgetting that he had a sword, knocking them both to the ground. Mackintosh was driven back by a French sergeant, who snatched his rifle and wrestled it to the side so the Scot couldn't shoot him.

Another Frenchman lunged at Plunket with his bayonet, and he knew they were seconds from being overwhelmed. The sergeant kicked Mackintosh's feet from under him, bowling him over, while another Frenchman stood poised to plunge his bayonet down into the grappling Fraser.

Then a shout went up, from the direction of the church. Workers were running from it, and they were armed. Plunket saw that Maria was among them.

It seemed Carlos's sister was not a secret servant of Napoleon after all.

The partisans caught the French from behind, attacking them with hammers and mallets and knives and a few clubbed muskets. One shot a Frenchman at point-blank range, the discharge threatening to ignite the man's woollen uniform, while another slashed the soldier about to run Fraser through. The French sergeant was brought down before he could strike at Mackintosh, beaten and broken. Maria rammed a broad-bladed butcher's knife into the side of the man fighting Plunket, and the rifleman took the opportunity to crack his weapon's stock against the man's head, sending his shako flying and putting him on the ground.

It was over as quickly as it had begun, but there was hardly time to take stock – more French infantry were rushing through the swelling crowd of workers at the dock, closing in on the little band from all across the parade square.

'*Vamos,*' Maria shouted, gesturing with her bloody knife towards the church.

'No,' Plunket said, dragging the wide-eyed Fraser to his feet and snapping at him to translate. 'Tell her that there's no hope of us killing Dubertrand today. She needs to get out and lie low. Don't give up!'

'What about us?' Mackintosh asked.

'Best we can do right now is provide a distraction,' Plunket said. 'Into the stable. The rest of you, go! *Vamos!*'

He waved the workers and partisans back into the alleyway, hoping they would be able to lose themselves in the chaos, then kicked the stable doors in.

Chapter Thirteen

Fort Josephine, Zaragoza, North-Eastern Spain, October 27th, 1809

WITHIN THE STABLE, all was dust and shadows. Mackintosh paused at the door and fired, bringing down a French officer trying to form and direct his men. Plunket moved inside, eyes adjusting to his new surroundings. The stalls were full on either side, their equine occupants snorting and stamping. The only person present was a stable boy who stared wide-eyed up at Plunket before fleeing towards a door in the back.

'The ladder, there,' Plunket said, indicating a way up into the hay loft that formed the stable's second tier. He pushed Fraser towards it.

'Lose the cloaks as well,' he instructed, pulling his own off and tossing it aside. There was no chance they were going to avoid capture now, and being taken in uniform was essential.

Mackintosh closed the stable doors and barred them, and the trio scrambled up to the second level.

'Look for a way onto the roof,' Plunket said. 'We needed to keep their attention on us for as long as possible.'

He knelt amidst the musty straw and began to reload as the other two hunted for a way higher up, pouring powder down his rifle's barrel before ramming home ball and patch and priming the pan.

There was a flurry of impacts as the French began beating at the door with fists and musket butts. It held only briefly before splintering, light spilling in.

Plunket was about to fire at the first man to come charging through, but Fraser's shout made him hesitate. He had located another short ladder leading to a hatch in the roof.

'Get up it,' Plunket barked at him. Mackintosh reloaded as well, as Fraser scrambled up and pushed open the hatch.

On impulse, Plunket darted further back into the loft, as deep into it as the straw heaped up towards its back would permit. Baker rifle at half cock, he shoved the weapon in amongst the fodder, dragging more down on top of it, before moving towards the hatch.

Mackintosh fired, the crash of the discharge loud in the confined space. One of the Frenchmen surging through the broken doorway was snatched back. Several returned fire up into the dusty, manure-stinking darkness, their bullets smacking splinters from the wood around the riflemen.

'Up,' Plunket urged Mackintosh. The Scotsman slung his rifle and pounded up the ladder. A bullet hit one of the rungs, splitting it.

Plunket doubled back and kicked the first ladder leading from the bottom floor away just as the first Frenchman had started to scale it, then scrambled back and up towards the hatch. He pulled himself out into the sunlight, finding Fraser and Mackintosh already trying to work their way unsteadily along a sloping timber roof towards the edge of the neighbouring church, now right beside them.

There were French soldiers in the alleyway below but, Plunket was glad to see, there was no sign of Maria and her partisans. The blue-coated infantry fired up at them, the air alive with the thrum and whistle of musket balls.

'Jump,' he shouted at Fraser and Mackintosh as he tried to catch up. The lieutenant hesitated, but the rifleman didn't, throwing himself at the opposite rooftop. He cleared the narrow alleyway and clattered into the red tiles, almost losing his grip on his rifle and having to snatch it by the sling.

'Go, damn it,' Plunket shouted at Fraser. With a strangled cry, the young lieutenant finally obeyed, following Mackintosh across.

A bullet, fired from below, passed so close to Plunket it nicked at his green jacket. Snarling, he squatted down and threw himself at the gap. There was a split second of plunging terror where he thought he wasn't going to make it, then he was against the tiles, grunting with pain as his elbow cracked against them, scrabbling for a handhold so he didn't slide back down into the abyss beneath.

Mackintosh grabbed at him and steadied him against the roofing of the church. It was partially collapsed; the central joists having fallen away when fire had burned out the structure's guts. The tower still stood though, its stonework scarred and blackened, a memoriam to the flame that had almost destroyed it.

The charred remnants of a doorway still stood in the tower's flank, allowing access from the church out onto the roof. The three made for it.

'See if we can get up top,' Plunket said to Mackintosh. 'You might still be able to get a shot.'

Any hope of holding out in the tower vanished after Fraser kicked in the blackened timber of the doorway. He found himself face to face with another Frenchman, who discharged his musket the same instant Fraser threw himself to the side.

The man charged out after him, bayonet levelled, and more followed, including an officer brandishing his sword and screaming at the three British soldiers.

Plunket looked back the way they had come, to the stable roof, but their pursuers had made it up there as well. Several made the jump across, cutting off even the route back along the church exterior.

They were surrounded. Plunket drew his sword bayonet, even though he knew it was useless. He wouldn't be taken without a weapon in hand.

Mackintosh clubbed his musket and held it up and away from his body, the sign of surrender, and after a moment Fraser reversed the sword he had finally remembered to draw, hesitatingly proffering its hilt to the French officer, who ceased his shouting and glared at the young Scot, before accepting the weapon.

'We surrender,' Fraser said as he gave it up, though the words came out choked. After the rush of flight, sudden inaction was clearly difficult.

Plunket felt no different. He had known this was the likely outcome as soon as Carlos had started drawing the garrison's attention, but now that it was happening it still stung, still made him burn with shame and frustration.

They had failed, and the deaths of Smith and Jones had been in vain.

The officer snapped something to his men, and they edged past along the rooftop, tiles scraping underfoot, several coming loose and clattering down into the alleyway below.

'Let them take you,' Plunket ordered Fraser, knowing that any resistance, even an accidental thrust against one of their captors along the precarious edge, would likely see them shot down in a hail of musketry.

Fraser and then Mackintosh were hauled towards the tower door. A French corporal, his rank signified by the two stripes just above his red cuff, batted Plunket's sword bayonet aside before snatching it. Plunket forced himself to relinquish the weapon.

They were taken down into the parade. The factory workers had been corralled close to the workhouses, a line of French infantry holding them at bayonet point. Others were lifting the bodies of those killed and laying them out in front of the stables. Plunket saw that the corpses of Carlos and Jones were there as well, side by side. The sight caused a fresh flare of anger, like the flash of gunpowder in a rifle's pan.

Plunket forced his attention back towards the penned-in factory workers but could see no immediate sign of Maria or the partisans who had saved them. That was the only good news – either they were successfully blending in among the workhands, or they had escaped outright.

The officer who had seized them spoke with another Frenchman, a major who was just hurrying onto the scene. The conversation was short but sharp, with the officer who had first captured them pointing repeatedly at the villa across the parade square. Eventually, the major seemed to relent and gestured for their captors to bring them.

They set off towards the villa, leaving the dead behind.

Chapter Fourteen

Fort Josephine, Zaragoza, North-Eastern Spain,
October 27th, 1809

DUBERTRAND HAD ORDERED that the three British prisoners be brought to his office.

'This is perhaps unwise, sir,' d'Arcy advised. 'They have likely been sent to kill you, after all.'

'Are you saying your men are not sufficient to protect me, despite the fact the prisoners have now been disarmed?' Dubertrand asked.

'No sir, only that unnecessary risks—'

Dubertrand stopped listening, instead watching the prisoners as they were brought in, looking equal parts curious and angry.

They had almost ruined everything, this ragged little band. It was vital that the gunpowder shipments went undisturbed – Dubertrand was under no illusions that his funding and the resources bestowed upon him by the emperor relied on the factory's ongoing production. Worse, the infiltrators had even been mad enough to discharge weapons within feet of the gunpowder barrels.

'You realise we could all have been killed earlier, and everything I have been working towards might have been destroyed?' Dubertrand said, focusing his attention, and his ire, back upon d'Arcy. 'This lapse in security is utterly unacceptable! How is it possible this even came to pass? We are hundreds of kilometres from where that little English army is squatting for the winter.'

'I informed you of the intelligence passed to me by

General Girard, that partisans have been seeking the help of the English,' d'Arcy said. 'Their intention was to strike at us here. One such group was intercepted just a few days ago. These are likely the survivors from that same expedition.'

'I cannot possibly squander attention on such matters, not while I am in the midst of my research,' Dubertrand exclaimed, snatching up a page of formulas from his desk and waving it in d'Arcy's face. 'That is why you are employed here, Major! To protect this fortress, its productivity, and *me!*'

'There has been a lapse,' d'Arcy admitted. 'It had been reported to me that the partisans had been wiped out well south of here. The individual who has been feeding us intelligence was apparently unable to forewarn us of this attempt to infiltrate the fort until the last minute. He paid for that failure with his life.'

'As he should,' Dubertrand said. 'I heard shooting from the workhouses as well. There are partisans there, too? Have they infiltrated the labourers?'

'It seems possible,' d'Arcy said. 'My men are searching the entire workforce as we speak. We can begin questioning—'

'There is no time, just search them and have any that are armed killed, then double the guards. I have already received a letter from General Girard promising more men!'

He looked back at the trio of captives now standing under guard before his desk.

'I am told, you came here to deprive France of my genius, by killing me,' he addressed them, putting his English to the test for the first time in years. None of the three showed any reaction. The two older ones, dressed in shabby green, simply stared straight ahead, displaying the sort of brutish, dull, animal-like mentality Dubertrand had come to associate with common soldiers. The third, though, wearing a bright red coat, was younger, and his obvious nervousness implied there was at least something functioning between his ears.

'You are an officer, yes?' Dubertrand asked the youth. 'Your uniform betrays it. I suppose I should be honoured that you were sent to kill me. Now I know that not only does my emperor appreciate my efforts here, but his enemies do as well.'

'He hasn't come here to kill you,' one of the green-clad ones spoke up, to Dubertrand's surprise. 'He speaks Spanish. He only came to translate between us and the partisans.'

'Is that so?' Dubertrand said, looking at the speaker with renewed interest. He was tall, dark-haired, with pallid blue eyes. Killer's eyes, Dubertrand thought.

'You have command then?' he asked the man, pacing out from behind his desk. 'What is your name?'

'Corporal Plunket,' came the reply, those eyes not blinking as they followed Dubertrand.

'A mere *caporal* was sent to kill me?'

Plunket said nothing. Dubertrand held his gaze with a ferocity of his own, then spoke to d'Arcy in French.

'Have them shot.'

'I cannot,' d'Arcy said. 'They were taken in uniform.'

'The one in red, perhaps, but these green rags are surely not uniforms?'

'They are riflemen.'

'Riflemen,' Dubertrand repeated, a little surprised. 'I have heard of the British use of rifles. Why does the emperor not equip any of his troops with such weapons? They are far more accurate than a common musket, are they not?'

'And slower to load,' d'Arcy said, his tone taking on a defensive edge. 'For every shot a rifleman makes, one of our *voltigeurs* can manage two or even three.'

'Better one bullet that hits than three that miss, no?' Dubertrand asked, enjoying the opportunity to needle at the army major. 'Surely there is a happy medium? Equipping a few of the best marksmen from each *voltigeur* company would not significantly reduce their firepower but would improve their accuracy. Or these English will be able to kill at range, unchallenged.'

'I do not presume to question the emperor's decisions,' d'Arcy said.

'Which is why you will never progress far in life, major,' Dubertrand told him. 'Now, uniforms or not, I want these three *rosbifs* shot. Or must I remind you who commands here, as I did with that miserable Spanish thief we caught in this very room?'

'It is against every rule of war—'

'In case you had failed to notice, Major, I am not one of your soldiers. I don't need to obey your petty little rules. I command here in a civilian capacity, by the will of the emperor himself!'

'If you want to murder these men, you can do it yourself,' d'Arcy said, fire in his eyes. That surprised Dubertrand and angered him.

'I will report you to General Girard for this insubordination,' he snarled. 'And to Paris, in my next communique! What is the name of your immediate subordinate?'

'Captain Marcelle,' d'Arcy said acidly.

'Then we shall see if Captain Marcelle is better at following orders,' Dubertrand snapped, before telling one of the guards to go and find the officer.

'Step forward, Plunket,' he then instructed the rifleman who had spoken to him before. The man did so, his expression defiant. Dubertrand commanded the guards on either side of him to snatch his right arm and force it against the desk. The rifleman resisted, until one of the guards passed his musket to another so he could properly grapple with the prisoner and pin him in place.

'You came here intending to shoot me, did you not?' Dubertrand demanded.

'I came here to bloody kill you,' Plunket snarled. Dubertrand grinned viciously at him, relishing the man's defiance, letting it feed his own simmering rage.

'I wonder how accurate you would be with your rifle, if you could not pull the trigger,' he said, before picking up the small bust of de Lavoisier sitting on the desk next to where his arm was pinned. Face contorting with fury, the chemist smashed the stone head down into the rifleman's hand one, two, three times, until he heard bone crunch and split.

To his gratification, Plunket cried out in pain. Only then did Dubertrand cease, his grip on the bust shaking, his eyes wild, a strand of silver hair hanging loose across his face.

'I think you will not be shooting me now, *Caporal* Plunket,' he snarled then, carefully, he placed the bust back down on his desk.

'Take them all away, throw them in the cells,' he ordered the guards, then spoke to D'Arcy, who was staring at him with horror.

'You are relieved of command, major,' he told him. 'Get out of my fort. We'll see if Captain Marcelle is more receptive to my orders.'

THE GUARDS TOOK Plunket, Fraser and Mackintosh down to the casemates on the west side of the fort. They were vaulted spaces, dug in beneath the walls and reinforced with stone. Their primary purpose was to store ammunition for the fort's artillery, though they also seemed to be serving as a place to keep excess gunpowder from the factory. A section of it, the British discovered, was also serving as a jail.

They were let through a barred metal grate and placed in a side room. Its only amenities were half a dozen rough wooden cots, with ratty blankets packed with stale straw, and a few foul-smelling buckets. The chamber was lit by the winter sunlight streaming in through a small, grated opening where the wall met the ceiling, presumably at the foot of the bastion the casement had been built into the base of.

'Reminds me of Enniscorthy gaol,' Plunket said as the door was slammed shut and locked behind them. He was trying not to let the pain in his right hand show. It had turned black and blue and started to swell monstrously. Worse, he couldn't move his right index and middle fingers.

He wouldn't be pulling a trigger with that hand anytime soon and knew it would be next to impossible to take an aimed shot with his left – every rifle's lock plate was on the right side of the stock, to ensure the flash from the pan was away from the firer's face. Even those who favoured their left hand over their right had to shoot with their right, or risk having the side of their head burned.

'Best get that bound up,' Mackintosh said, looking at the injured hand. He moved to one of the beds, tearing the bottom part off a blanket.

'Might hurt a wee bit,' he said as he returned and began to bind the injured hand into a makeshift sling that he tied over one shoulder. Plunket gritted his teeth but couldn't stop a hiss of pain from escaping.

'Guessing that was Dubertrand then,' Mackintosh said as he worked. 'Can't imagine why anyone would possibly want to put a bullet in him.'

'Sometimes, duty and pleasure align,' Plunket growled, looking across at Fraser. The young officer hadn't spoken a word since they had been taken, and was now standing, pale-faced, in the small beam of sunlight entering in through the hole at the top of the wall, gazing up into it.

'You're not hurt, are you?' Plunket asked, trying to get his attention, wondering if he had missed an injury to the lieutenant during the chaos of their failed escape.

Fraser blinked, and looked at Plunket, as though seeing him for the first time.

'They're going to shoot us,' he said abruptly.

'What?' Mackintosh asked, pausing his tying of the sling.

'I speak French,' Fraser admitted. 'Enough to get the gist of what they were saying back in the villa. The one dressed as a civilian, Dubertrand, he ordered the officer to have us shot.'

'We're prisoners of war,' Mackintosh said. 'They can't.'

'Not sure that chemist much cares about the rules of war,' Plunket said, nodding down at his hand.

'There has to be something we can do,' Fraser said, sounding as though he was starting to panic. 'They could come back at any minute! I'm telling you; they're going to kill us!'

'Well, any suggestions you might have would be more than welcome, sir,' Mackintosh replied with only a sliver of sarcasm.

Plunket had already been considering their options. Currently, they looked non-existent. The grate was clearly securely fastened, and there were two guards directly outside. He had counted more on the heavy oak doors leading into the casement, and yet more immediately outside. It made sense, with the gunpowder stored so nearby, that this part of the fort would be crawling with soldiers.

The only immediate hope Plunket could conceive of was that Maria and her partisans had evaded capture – maybe their absence from the cell was a good sign, assuming this was the only secure holding place in the fort. He doubted the French could afford to fully interrogate all of the factory workers or simply eject them out into the town, not when they were still in the middle of loading the barges. From their brief interaction, Dubertrand didn't seem like someone who would accept delays, or drops in productivity.

Perhaps, if Maria was still free, she would make an effort to break them out. But then, considering what had happened at the wharves, Plunket knew he couldn't rely on anyone outside the cell.

'We were betrayed,' he said bitterly.

'We knew it had to be one of them who warned the frogs,' Mackintosh pointed out.

'But El Cruz was killed during that ambush,' Fraser said. 'Would Carlos see his own father shot down by the very people who invaded his home?'

'He had already betrayed the rest of his countrymen, why stop at his own family?' Mackintosh said. 'At least his sister doesn't seem to have been in on it.'

'*Afrancesado*,' Fraser said coldly. Plunket raised an eyebrow.

'Spaniards who sympathise with the French,' the officer elaborated. 'El Cruz said his son had studied in Paris. He must have picked up revolutionary, or Bonapartist ideology.'

'And now it's got him killed,' Mackintosh said. 'Him and plenty of others besides.'

Plunket thought again about Smith, and now Jones, lying abandoned out there. He had little doubt that by tomorrow the Welshman's body would have been tossed indiscriminately into a mass grave somewhere nearby.

Perhaps the rest of them would be tossed in there too, if Fraser was right about what Dubertrand had ordered.

'We're just lucky we didn't let Carlos skedaddle to the fort earlier, or we would have been taken long before those barges made it to the jetties,' he thought aloud.

'He still did his job, did he not?' Fraser pointed out, the despair returning. 'We're as good as dead here. Hundreds of miles from the duke's army. From any kind of help.'

'If there's going to be any help, I don't think our army is going to have a great deal to do with it,' Plunket replied.

THEY WAITED. FRASER did his best not to let the fear that was gnawing at him show, resisting the urge to pace up and down the cell. He sat on the end of one of the crude beds instead and tried to run through all that had happened in his mind, trying to decide whether he was at fault for where they now found themselves.

Should he have foreseen Carlos's treachery? Plunket certainly had his suspicions, but as the one who had been brought specifically to liaise with the Spanish, Fraser couldn't help but feel responsible. He should have paid more attention during the journey to Zaragoza, even tried to ingratiate himself with the partisans. Perhaps he could have caught or overheard something, some hint that would have pointed towards Carlos, and impending disaster.

That would have been difficult to do given the disdain the Spanish had displayed from the moment they had learned Plunket's identity. Why would no one tell him the root of that antagonism? He could forgive the riflemen some of their brusque, dismissive attitude towards him, even if it was no way for rankers to interact with an officer – he accepted that he was inexperienced, perhaps even outright unsuited to this deadly new world he had thrown himself into so eagerly. But how could he be expected to provide genuine assistance to their mission when he was treated as little better than a child, an encumbrance barely tolerated by either the riflemen or the guerillas?

On an impulse born out of frustration, Fraser rose from the bed and went and stood in front of Plunket.

'Why does Lieutenant Colonel Robertson hate you?' he asked. The rifleman didn't deign to look at him, let alone answer.

Fraser felt his anger rising, slow but steady, taking the place of the despair that had gripped him.

'And the Spaniards too,' he pressed, his voice growing louder. 'They spoke as though they knew you and despised you. Yet no one will explain it. Why won't anybody tell me the truth?'

'That's enough, lad,' Mackintosh interrupted. 'The corporal's in no mood to—'

'It's fine,' Plunket said suddenly, to both their surprise. 'The boy might as well know. It was Buenos Aires. The capital of the place the Spaniards call the Viceroyalty of the Río de la Plata. A long bloody way from here, though not so different in many ways.'

'You were part of the 1807 expedition, under Sir William Beresford,' Fraser said, sensing that, at last, Plunket wanted to talk. 'I know the 95th were part of that force. One of their first campaigns.'

'It was nearly our last as well,' Mackintosh said when Plunket didn't respond. 'We thought we'd been through hell. Then, a year later, we ended up with Moore's army in Galicia. That was real suffering.'

'They were both real suffering,' Plunket said bitterly.

'You fought the Spanish, before they became our allies,' Fraser said, slowly beginning to understand.

'It was more than that,' Plunket said. 'And seeing as, according to you, we're now little better than dead men, you might as well hear the story of it. The whole damned, sorry tale.'

Chapter Fifteen

Buenos Aires, Viceroyalty of the Río de la Plata, South America, July 5th, 1807

'LEFT SIDE OF the street, the second window on the right, above the draper's shop.'

Plunket followed Mackintosh's directions and located the window he was talking about, and the man who was leaning out of it, musket pointed down towards the redcoats holding the barricade in the street below.

The greenjacket shifted in his own perch amidst the rubble of the church steeple, angling his Baker rifle towards the window across the square. Both Plunket and the new-acquired target were high enough up to not be inhibited by the smoke rising from the battle raging below, and there was no wind to speak of. Plunket lined up, resting the barrel on the edge of the broken wall, the leaf of the rear sight raised to account for the target being a little under two hundred yards distant.

He eased the breath from his lungs and fired.

The smoke obscured the target, but Plunket was already reloading anyway.

'A hit,' Mackintosh growled. 'That's your seventeenth.'

The numbers were becoming meaningless, the kills a blur. The battle had been raging all day – it had been hours since they had taken up their current position, in the remains of a steeple belonging to a tall, whitewashed church dominating the southern side of a city square. The steeple's top had been partially demolished by artillery fire in the fighting that morning as the British pushed towards the confluence of streets, but enough of its uppermost floor – now mostly exposed to the outside – was still sufficiently intact for the pair of riflemen to use it as a perch.

More greenjackets occupied lower windows and the balcony that ran along the church's upper facade, commanded by Major Robertson. They had been firing in support of the British forces pinned along the edge of the square and the street leading into it all afternoon.

After the fifteenth kill, Plunket had swapped his rifle for Mackintosh's. The repeated firings had left the weapon too fouled with gunpowder residue to reload without great difficulty, and the barrel was scorching hot to the touch.

Another ten or so shots and Mackintosh's rifle would be in a no better state. Hot water could be used to sluice and clean it, but they barely had a drop left in their canteens to drink, let alone see to the weapons – Plunket's throat was parched and his lips chapped. The only blessing was that loading with his powder horn and patched ball meant he wasn't having to bite into paper cartridges, meaning the gunpowder residue wasn't adding to his thirst. He couldn't imagine the struggles of the redcoat infantry below.

The only other alternative was to piss down the barrel, an act sometimes undertaken by riflemen in desperate circumstances. Current circumstances were more than desperate, but when Mackintosh had offered to do so with the fouled rifle, Plunket had told him to stay where he was – he needed him focused on the square and its surroundings, picking out the most vital targets amidst the mass of smoke and flame and churning bodies while Plunket loaded and fired, as methodical as a machine.

The whole place looked like a scene from hell, like one of the dreadful, dark paintings that had used to scare Plunket in the chapel in Enniscorthy. The old artwork had depicted the inferno, the eternal torment that awaited sinners that did not confess and repent. He supposed it was apt – the whole expedition had gone to hell, and he feared none of them would be long in following it there.

It had started well enough. Plunket and the rest of the 95th had sailed with the fleet from England in October the year before, bound for the far climes of South America. They had discovered enroute that they were set to strike a blow against the Spanish colony of the Río de la Plata. As was so often the case, Spain had fallen in with France in its war against Britain, and some bright spark at Horse Guards had convinced everyone else that the best use of the army's precious manpower was striking an enemy colony halfway across the globe.

For the past six months the 95th had fought across the humid climes, from the storming of Montevideo in February to Colonia del Sacramento and the vicious skirmishing around San Pedro. Now, the final assault on Buenos Aires was underway, but the previous successes of the expedition had evaporated. The town's citizens had joined the Spanish soldiery in resisting the British advance, piling up barricades and fighting from one street to another. The offensive had rapidly become bogged down, and now the main British column was pinned behind those barricades they had captured in front of a square near the centre of the town. The enemy were closing in from every side, but still, the redcoats and their green-jacketed riflemen fought on.

'Officer, down by the statue, he's waving his hat about,' Mackintosh said. Plunket, who had just finished priming the rifle's pan, peered over the edge of the shattered steeple, locating first the landmark – a handsome fountain whose stone figures had been scarred and brutalised by musket balls and canister – and then the figure in question, a Spanish officer, regular army rather than the militia and private citizen volunteers who were resisting the British incursion so fiercely. He was wearing a white coat, edged with gold lace and, as Mackintosh had said, was seeking to marshal his nearby men by standing up on the edge of the fountain's bowl and waving his hat in one hand and his sword in the other. It was an unwise thing to do with a church full of riflemen across the square, and Plunket decided to ensure the man discovered his mistake too late.

He took aim. The light infantry school at Shorncliffe barracks taught weapons accuracy, but Plunket had required little in the way of training in that department. He had been shooting for as long as he could remember, stalking game with his father, until the lord who employed him had thrown them out one hard winter, when the gamekeeper had deliberately avoided reporting a few of his kills to make sure he could feed his family. The family had eventually found work in one of the new linen factories, but Plunket had refused to follow them into such drudgery. He had enlisted instead, enamoured by the dark green uniforms of a recruiting party from the 95th Rifles, who spoke of their newly founded regiment and how it prioritised quick thinkers and good shots over the mindless, brutally enforced discipline of the line regiments.

Now he was half the world away and fighting for his life.

He started reloading again but spared a glance up as he fished out a fresh, greased patch. There was no longer any sign of the officer he had fired at amidst the tumult.

'Going to need more patches and balls off you,' he told Mackintosh. He had started the engagement with a dozen pairs of both laid out next to one another on the wall beside him, but they were long gone. Besides the eighteen hits, he'd missed about a dozen and was down to his last few rounds.

Mackintosh passed him a fistful of loose balls, followed by his own patches, and his powder flask for good measure. He had settled into supporting Plunket without anything other than joking complaint – Plunket knew the Scot was a fine shot, but in the two years the pair of them had been with the 95th, no one had scored higher than him on the ranges. No one had even come close.

'Officer on a horse, just cantering in from the street directly opposite,' Mackintosh said, before adding a vehement expletive.

Plunket looked down once again into the maelstrom and saw the reason for his companion's curse. There was indeed a horseman riding into the square from the far side, but they weren't the main concern – it was the fact that there were five pieces of artillery being wheeled in his wake, along with limbers and caissons. The guns weren't especially large – brass-barrelled, probably three-pounders, Plunket thought – but their presence would surely tip the engagement in favour of the Spaniards. The British hadn't been able to get any similar guns this deep into the town, and the square offered the enemy the perfect opportunity to deploy them, outside the range of the redcoats still holding the barricades.

The cannons were wheeled by their crews into a firing line facing towards the southern side of the square. The officer on horseback was directing them, and he had wisely ordered them to deploy as far back from the church as possible – the range wasn't impossible for the riflemen, but it was far enough to make the shots unreliable.

Plunket took that as a challenge. He lined up on the officer.

'Waste of powder and ball?' Mackintosh muttered, seeing where Plunket was aiming.

'We need to do something,' he replied tersely. He fired.

There was a brief pause, before Mackintosh said 'nineteen.'

The Spanish gunners started to load, ramming ammunition down the barrels of their guns. Other riflemen were firing from lower down, but their shots were mostly falling short or missing their marks.

Plunket grunted as he rammed the next round home. The barrel was becoming increasingly clogged, slowing down the reloading process. That couldn't be helped. Speed and weight of fire were the prerogative of the smoothbore-armed line infantry. Aimed, accurate shots were the priorities of the greenjackets. Plunket didn't disparage the Brown Bess carried by the redcoats – despite the way some of the other riflemen talked about it. He had seen that weapon kill at two hundred yards, a shot that would have made any of the 95th proud. But two years on from the day he had first been issued it, he wouldn't swap his Baker Rifle for the world.

He took aim at one of the artillerists stooping behind his gun, setting the cannon's alignment on the church. He fired.

'Twenty,' Mackintosh said, sounding almost grudging.

As Plunket began reloading again, hands working his firearm automatically, he noticed the ferocious noise of the battle had started to die down. He exchanged a glance with Mackintosh, then risked another look over the wall and down into the centre of the square.

The Spanish infantry and militia pressing their assault on the redcoat barricades had started to pull back. It was clearly not because they were being driven back by sheer weight of firepower. They were attempting to clear the line of sight for the newly arrived battery.

'There's going to be hell to pay when those guns open up,' Plunket growled, urgently resuming his reloading.

Someone, somewhere, had ordered the redcoats to cease fire as the Spanish retreated to the far side of the square, and the command filtered through to the riflemen. A sudden quiet started to settle over the bloody scene. Plunket finished reloading, but kept still, he and Mackintosh peering down at what was playing out below them.

As the Spanish infantry formed ranks on either side of their newly unmasked artillery, a pair of officers on horseback cantered forward into the corpse-strewn space between the opposing sides. One was carrying a short pole aloft – around its top was a piece of white cloth.

'Flag of truce,' Mackintosh observed. 'Guess they want to parlay. Or want us to up and surrender, before those guns open up.'

A sudden, ferocious anger gripped Plunket, as hot as the midsummer sun beating down on them. They had come all this way, fought for weeks, sometimes tooth-and-nail, and now the Spanish believed they would simply surrender? The whole force, marched into shameful captivity, their flags and guns given up, the swords of their commanders yielded to their prideful enemies?

'Hold your fire,' he heard Major Robertson reiterating to the riflemen in the church below. Expression dark, Plunket slowly slid his Baker rifle over the wall's edge and took aim at the officer with the white flag.

'What're you doing, lad?' Mackintosh hissed, but Plunket ignored him. Others might think the situation was hopeless, but he wasn't going to surrender. He wasn't going to suffer the indignity or admit that those who had died for this hare-brained, stupid damn campaign had done so in vain. He wasn't going to yield his rifle to anyone.

He fired.

The shot sounded, a single, sharp crack in the stillness that had gripped the square.

Even as he squeezed the trigger, Plunket knew what he had done was madness. Even as the flame spat and the ball flew, he regretted it.

The shot took the Spaniard in the thigh. He clutched it and tumbled from his mount, blood spattering his white flag with a dash of bright crimson. The other officer wheeled his horse and cantered hard back towards his lines, leaving his fallen comrade behind. Several infantrymen, braver than their fleeing officer, ran forward to help the wounded man back to their ranks.

For a terrible fraction of time, all was silent and still, and Plunket dared to hope that the mistake he had just made would not prove fatal.

It was a fool's hope, to go with his foolish action, and it was proven as such when a voice rang out from amongst the enemy.

Then, the Spanish battery spoke.

The discharge was like a thunderclap, kicking up dust and debris from the cobbles and making the ruined structure around Plunket shiver. He threw himself down and heard the brutal cracking sound of canister whipping at the church steeple, throwing up powdered stone all around him and Mackintosh.

Two of the Spanish guns had discharged at the church, but the other three had sent their ordinance into the barricades. They didn't fire canister, but round shot, the solid iron balls crashing through the rough mounds of commandeered carts, doors, shutters and furniture, splintering them to pieces and carrying on through the red-coated men huddled behind. It transformed them into butcher's meat, and hideously gouged and lacerated others with the shards of wood from the very barricades they had been using as shelter.

As the echoes of the terrible bombardment clapped back from the surrounding buildings, Plunket made to rise up and return fire, but Mackintosh snatched him by his shoulder strap and yanked him back down.

'Think you've done enough, lad,' the Scotsman said.

The Spanish gunners knew their trade. Less than thirty seconds, and the gun crews had reloaded. More balls, blasted from the tin canisters like massive shotguns, whipped and scarred the facade of the church and cut down any rifleman caught exposed. At least others were able to find cover behind the stone walls – for the redcoats out on the street there was none, the barricades no protection. Round shot carved bloody furrows through them, and all they could do was endure.

Plunket stayed down, huddled beneath the wall as it was whipped and beaten by the Spanish guns. He felt anger every bit as potent as that crashing artillery, but even greater was the shame; shame at the knowledge he had violated a truce, even greater shame at the knowledge that the slaughter was his fault. He had lost control, and now dozens of men were being maimed and killed, the same men he counted as comrades, who he had voyaged with to this distant, burning land, who he had fought alongside these long, hard weeks. He stayed down, he listened to their screams beneath the hammering of the guns, and he wondered if this was the hell he had heard the priest speak of when he was a boy.

Whether it was or not, he knew his life would never be the same again.

Chapter Sixteen

Fort Josephine, Zaragoza, North-Eastern Spain, October 28th, 1809

FRASER SAT IN silence, and Plunket let it stretch. He felt suddenly exhausted, as though he had relived those terrible days minute by minute, blow for blow. He tried so often to forget, to put the horror of what he had unleashed behind him but knew in truth that he never would. It stayed with him, burned into his mind with utter clarity. Even after enduring the likes of the retreat to Corunna, it was Buenos Aires that haunted his nightmares and turned his waking thoughts cold and bitter.

'What happened after that?' Fraser asked eventually, his voice quiet.

Plunket finished the tale, telling of how the Spanish guns had eventually fallen silent, and their infantry had advanced to accept the unconditional surrender of the torn and broken remnants of the British expeditionary force. Nearly half the army had been killed or wounded.

While they were giving up their rifles, Major Robertson had demanded to know who among the 95th had shot the officer with the flag of truce. Plunket had admitted to it and, in a fit of fury, Robertson had struck him. He had found no reply. The icy looks of the other surviving riflemen had been a more stinging blow.

Most of the survivors had been allowed to return home, but a number had been taken into captivity. Plunket had volunteered for the duty, though he had known it would not atone him. Mackintosh had stayed as well, until the shifting tides of war had turned Spain from Britain's enemy into her ally. The prisoners had been released, and Plunket and the others had rejoined the ranks of the 95th just in time for the campaigns in Iberia.

'That's why Robertson dislikes you so,' Fraser said when Plunket was done. 'And the Spaniards. They knew what had happened in Buenos Aires.'

Plunket offered no reply.

'It wasn't you who killed those lads there,' Mackintosh said eventually. 'It was the Spaniards. And if you're looking for blame among our own, blame the likes of General Whitelock and Popham, and all the other arrogant bastards that led us out there to be killed.'

Plunket had heard it all before. He'd tried to accept it, to find agreement in Mackintosh's arguments, to see it as anything other than an attempt at absolving him of the blame he was due.

'It wasn't Whitelock or Popham who shot that officer with the white flag,' he said coldly.

'But think how many lives you've saved since,' Mackintosh said. 'You stopped the French advance at Cacabelos, for starters. The whole rearguard might have collapsed if those hussars had forced the bridge and broken through.'

'Is that why you fight so hard?' Fraser asked. 'Why you're so relentless? Because you think you still have to make up for what you did? You still have a debt to pay?'

'It's not a debt,' Plunket snarled. 'Only a burden. And there's nothing I can do to lighten it.'

He turned away, stalking to the corner of the cell and sitting with his back to the wall. His broken hand throbbed painfully. He was in no mood to talk anymore. Thankfully, it seemed neither were the others anyway. They let him be.

* * *

DURING THE EVENING, the guards brought them food – a cold stew and bread, and watered-down wine. That at least was probably a good sign. It seemed they weren't going to be executed until the morning.

They slept, shivering in the cold that settled throughout the fortress's stone depths. Plunket woke just before the dawn and watched the new day bleed in through the grate and spread across the straw-littered flagstones.

It was the first time he had shared what had happened in Buenos Aires with anyone outside the 95th. It had left a sour taste in his mouth, but while he had been speaking there had been a sense of relief, a sort of clarity that existed only in the moment. It was a reckoning with sin, he supposed, like when his father had made him attend the confessional. That strange, almost ethereal experience, sitting in the dark wooden box addressing one who was unseen, had always felt like an unburdening, even if all he was doing was admitting to poaching a rabbit or striking the miller's son, with whom he had skirmished with incessantly as a child. They had felt like grave enough crimes at the time.

To his credit, Fraser had displayed as little judgement as the black-clothed priest behind his wooden screen, showing none of the disgust Plunket had expected. The young officer just seemed thankful to have finally been taken into his confidence.

Perhaps Plunket should have spoken up to others before. Still, he doubted they would be so understanding. He was a killer and, worse, he had got his comrades killed, and those who survived more brutally treated than they otherwise might have been. The men of the regiment – the only family he had known since he had left Ireland – had every reason to despise him, to hate him as much as those Spaniards who knew the story of the rifleman who had violated a flag of truce. Yet not all did. Men like

Smith and Jones and Mackintosh had stood by him, and others besides. They could easily have left him for dead or even turned on him during the nightmare of the retreat to Corunna. Instead, they had held fast by his side, just as he had done his best to stick by them in turn.

Those two shots at Cacabelos had helped make the difference. He recalled the words he had spoken to Mackintosh before they had set out for Zaragoza, words he had been forced to live by ever since Buenos Aires.

The army finds me useful, so I need to keep being useful.

The daylight grew stronger. Plunket lay, shutting out the cold, watching, listening, waiting. He was expecting the door to grind open, for the guards to snatch them from their beds and haul them out, to stand them in front of the wall outside. A dawn firing squad, the fate of spies and assassins, and murderers.

It was only fitting, he supposed.

Eventually, he caught the sounds he had been expecting – footsteps, the jangle of keys. Mackintosh and Fraser stirred as he threw off his blanket and stood.

French soldiers entered, bayonets poised, and so, too, did a man Plunket recognised – the French major who had taken them to the villa, and had seemed to argue with Dubertrand. The dawn light caught the man's features as he paused to survey the sorry trio of captives.

'Let's get it over with then, Frenchie,' Mackintosh growled at him.

'My name is Major Charles D'Arcy,' the man responded in good English. 'You will accompany me to the gatehouse.'

None of them moved.

'Why the gatehouse?' Plunket asked warily.

'I intend to turn you over to the commander of the wider Zaragoza garrison, General Girard,' d'Arcy said. 'You will go into his custody, rather than *Monsieur* Dubertrand's.'

Nobody said anything, until Plunket asked the obvious question.

'Why?'

A brief grimace passed over d'Arcy's face, before an expression of stolid professionalism reasserted itself.

'In brief, you have already encountered *Monsieur* Dubertrand. The power he has been given here is... unprecedented. His orders bring shame upon the army and the country to which I have pledged my life, like my father before me. I will not dishonour myself or the men under my command by permitting your execution. There have been enough of those already. But Dubertrand's control only extends within the confines of this fort. That is why I am removing you from it.'

'So you're going to let us rot in a prison cell instead,' Plunket surmised.

'General Girard is a man of honour, as little pleased with the chemist's presence as I am. He will not mistreat you, nor return you to this place. You will be held as prisoners of war. For that, you should be thankful.'

Plunket was, though he wouldn't admit it. It still felt like some kind of trap, almost a cruel joke given all he had admitted to Fraser.

'I take it Dubertrand doesn't know you're doing this?' he asked.

'Not yet,' d'Arcy admitted.

'Don't you worry about what he'll do when he finds out you've transferred prisoners rather than executed them?'

'He may already have forgotten you,' d'Arcy said, though he sounded doubtful. 'He is obsessed with his work. Regardless, the worst he could do is have me removed from this post, and that is something I would more than welcome. Protecting this brute and enacting his cruel whims is not the reason I joined the army.'

Plunket nodded, satisfied. It was a damn sight better than what he had been expecting.

The guards closed in, and the trio were marched from the cell and up, out of the casement. The parade square was deserted, bathed in wintery morning sunlight.

D'Arcy and two guards led them across it, towards the gatehouse that lay at the far eastern end of the fort, facing into Zaragoza. Plunket was surprised at how few guards there were, but supposed d'Arcy had orchestrated it that way deliberately. For all the fact that he intended to hand them over to the town garrison for imprisonment, he was still essentially springing them from jail. If he was caught in the act, Plunket suspected his fate would be somewhat worse than simple reassignment or demotion.

They neared the tangle of workhouses and stables close to the church on the eastern side of the fort. There was no sign of the bodies laid out there anymore, but Plunket could still see the blood, dark and dry on the cobbles.

D'Arcy hurried their pace. The route to the gatehouse led them between the workhouses, the rough-hewn facades of the wooden buildings seeming to glare down at them, windows still shuttered, blind and cold.

Plunket was about to ask what had happened to the workers after yesterday, but the sounds of running feet interrupted him. One of the guards let out a cry, and he saw there were figures rushing in from the alleyways on either side, cloaked, with rags drawn up over their faces.

D'Arcy shouted something in French, but it was too late. The men were upon them, wielding hammers and blades – the factory workers, returned again when he had least expected them.

The two guards weren't enough. They went down fast and remarkably quietly, neither managing to discharge their firearms. D'Arcy had drawn his sword, steel whispering from its scabbard, but there were too many –

one slammed a wooden mallet into his ribs from behind, another kicked at his ankle, and bore the French officer down, like the wild, starved dogs that Plunket had seen following the raggedy army through Galicia, waiting to savage any stragglers who lagged behind.

'Wait,' Plunket barked, thrusting back one Spaniard as he stood over d'Arcy, the morning light glinting from his drawn knife. The man turned on Plunket with a snarl, but another figure put a hand on his shoulder, quietening him.

She tugged her mask down, and Plunket saw it was Maria, fire in her eyes, her own blade red and dripping.

She began to say something to Plunket, but he spoke over her to Fraser.

'Tell them he isn't to be harmed,' he said, standing over d'Arcy and glaring from one Spaniard to another. 'He was taking us out of the damned fort.'

'Maria says if they don't kill him, he'll raise the alarm,' Fraser said.

'Then we take him with us, as a prisoner,' Plunket ordered.

There was no time for further translation – a shout came from the direction of the gatehouse, followed by a gunshot, startlingly loud in the quiet morning, reverberating back from the tall buildings.

There were French soldiers coming from the fort's entrance. The partisans scattered, grabbing Plunket, Mackintosh and Fraser as they went, drawing them into the alleyways and leaving d'Arcy on his knees in the street, untouched.

Chapter Seventeen

Fort Josephine, Zaragoza, North-Eastern Spain, October 28th, 1809

PLUNKET ALLOWED HIMSELF to be led along. The partisans must have been watching for an opportunity like this, he thought. That, or they had informants of their own among the enemy's ranks.

One of the Spaniards opened a side door into the workhouse they were passing by, and ushered them in. Plunket could hear Frenchmen shouting from out in the street, and the sound of hobnails clattering on cobbles. He ducked into the shadows.

Within was a dingy hallway of timber boards, light edging past the shutters barring the windows. A staircase rose up to the right, but the partisans led them on, to what looked like a pantry. Shelves were stocked with jars and crates, but they were not the objective of the Spaniards. Maria ushered them to one side and drew up the ratty rug covering the floor. Floorboards followed, pried apart to reveal a hole, with worn stone steps leading down into a deeper and more foreboding darkness.

Candles were taken from piles on a shelf and lit with a striking flint. Maria and several other partisans began to descend, before waving the British after them.

Plunket exchanged a brief glance with Fraser and Mackintosh, then followed.

They went carefully down into the dark. It grew far more absolute when those partisans who had remained behind replaced the floorboards above them. Suddenly all they had was the candlelight, throwing a flickering luminescence over the bare earth and timber struts supporting the passageway.

The place was steep, narrow, and smelled old. Plunket found himself reminded once again of the confessional box: musty, quiet, brooding. Saturated with sin, with admissions of guilt that had bled over the centuries into the very woodwork.

He thrust the comparison from his mind.

Fraser almost lost his footing, and Mackintosh had to dart an arm out to steady him. It was difficult going for Plunket, with one arm in a sling – he put out his other hand against the wall to help guide himself.

They reached the bottom, emerging into a large cellar, supported by timber beams. Racks along one wall held a wooden framework supporting barrels, casks, and bottles, all dusty with age.

'Well, bless me,' Fraser murmured as they looked about.

It was a wine cellar. Not the sort of thing he had been expecting a hastily constructed labour workhouse to contain.

The partisans moved through it, apparently checking that they were alone, before those with candles secured them in cobwebbed sconces around the chamber.

It was older than the workhouse, Plunket thought, a cellar belonging to a structure that had once stood on the same site, and upon whose foundations the newer buildings within Fort Josephine had been constructed. A tavern perhaps, or a villa like the one opposite. The whole fort had been built over the western extremes of the town. Here, the partisans had found a place that the French quite probably had no idea existed.

The ability of Maria and her partisans to go undiscovered within the defences now made more sense.

He began to say as much, but Maria hushed him. In the silence that followed, he detected what she was listening for – it was the sound of a bell, tolling somewhere above.

'*La alarma,*' she said quietly.

They were being hunted. Briefly, Plunket wondered what had become of Major d'Arcy.

Maria spoke again, and Fraser translated.

'We need to remain down here until the search ceases,' Fraser told Plunket. He looked at the young woman as he spoke.

'How did you know we'd be taken from the jail?'

'They thought you would be shot and were going to try and strike before the execution took place,' Fraser said as she replied to him.

'They weren't going to shoot us, damn it. They were taking us from the fort.'

'She wants to know why they would release you.'

'Not releasing, transferring,' Plunket said, wondering how he could explain d'Arcy's stated intentions without making the situation sound suspicious. 'The commander of the Zaragoza garrison wanted to interrogate us.'

'*Afortunado*,' Maria said after a lingering look.

'Your brother betrayed us,' Plunket said, not caring that there was a sharp edge to his words. The death of Jones, and their wider failure to reach Dubertrand, were all still raw.

'She says he is not her brother anymore,' Fraser said as Maria spat a reply, her anger clashing with her desire to stay quiet. 'She says he died when her father sent him off to Paris. The French filled his head with their poison and lies.'

'And she only realised that when he started calling the guards down on us?' Plunket asked pointedly.

'If she had wanted to betray you too, she would have done so by now,' Fraser said, clearly uncomfortable acting as the conversation's mediator. 'She would have warned the French sooner, and would not have come back for us, and would not have led us down here, to safety.'

Plunket knew that was true enough, but he had wanted to vent his anger at Carlos's betrayal and had wanted to make sure the *afrancesado's* sister was truly on their side.

'And where is here?' he asked. Fraser listened to Maria's reply and appeared to ask a few questions before giving Plunket the answer.

'Upstairs used to be a wine seller's shop. It burned during the fighting at the start of the year, but when the French ordered the fort constructed, the builders made sure the cellar was hidden. It is the same with other structures inside the fort.'

'There are more cellars?'

'Yes, and some buried crypts under the church. She says they have been working to dig out a passage between there and here.'

Plunket was about to reply, but Maria hushed him again with a sharp, chopping gesture.

He heard voices, coming from above. French, accompanied by muffled footsteps. There was a creak from the top of the stairs.

A French soldier was standing right over the false boards.

They stood in frozen silence, gazing up into the darkness, breath held. Plunket found himself wishing he had a weapon to hand.

Eventually, the pressure on the floorboards ceased, and the voices receded again. They dared to breathe once more.

'Swear to me that you knew nothing of your brother's betrayal,' Plunket said to Maria once he was sure the French had departed.

'I don't think we're in much of a position to alienate the lassie,' Mackintosh pointed out quietly, but Plunket would not back down.

'She told me before she would rather cut her own throat than betray her people,' he said. 'So tell her to swear, Fraser, on her family and her honour and on God, if she still believes in the divine. Swear she didn't know what Carlos was planning, and that she won't turn against us.'

Plunket had expected more anger, more outrage and defiance, but instead Maria's expression became grave, almost solemn as she listened to Fraser's haltingly made demand. She exchanged a brief conversation with the lieutenant then, to Plunket's further surprise, spoke the two words in English.

'I swear.'

He knew he would have to be satisfied. Maria seemed as disgusted by her brother's betrayal as he was. He thought again about the argument he had overheard the siblings having when they had first set out. Carlos had been trying to convince his sister to abandon the expedition, knowing that a trap had already been set for them, but unable to admit as much to her. Maria wouldn't have countenanced helping the French if she had known what he had done.

'We're still on the same side then,' he told her. 'And I still have a mission to complete.'

The young partisan responded by turning away and issuing a series of hushed orders. Several of her men moved to the racks supporting the casks, barrels and wine bottles and, as quietly as possible, started to open them. Plunket soon saw why.

The barrels were filled not with wine, but with weapons. The guerillas revealed a stack of muskets, then sacks filled with paper cartridges – ammunition, bearing powder and ball. It was an eclectic mix, the weapons a combination of Spanish military firearms and what looked like civilian guns and fowling pieces, and there were also a few pistols and a rough assortment of hand-to-hand weapons, from knives and bayonets to clubs and hammers. The casks were quietly emptied of the deadly array, which was laid out on several blankets spread on the dusty floor. The candlelight winked on keen edges and steel barrels.

'Not exactly going to rearm the whole Spanish army,' Mackintosh noted with a hint of humour. 'But it's a start, I suppose.'

'How many of the workforce are actually willing to fight?' Plunket asked Maria.

'Enough,' came the reply, through Fraser. 'They have been waiting for this opportunity. Working towards it. Praying for it.'

Plunket thought for a moment, before nodding.

'Then she can tell them, when she next gets the opportunity, that their prayers are about to be answered.'

Chapter Eighteen

Fort Josephine, Zaragoza, North-Eastern Spain, October 28th, 1809

DUBERTRAND HISSED THROUGH his teeth with frustration, then crumpled the paper he had been scribbling on in his fist.

He had been so close. A rush of equations, a confluence of possibilities he had never considered before, all lost, all smashed to irreparable splinters by the clanging of that damned bell.

He rose from behind his desk and looked out of the window. Fort Josephine's square lay before him, the jetties further to his right busy with activity as workers sought to fill the waiting fleet of barges with the produce of the fort's factory. The work had been curtailed yesterday by the surprise attack of the Englishmen, and the details assigned to the loading had only just got back to work. Such inefficiencies distressed Dubertrand deeply, especially as he knew it would reflect back negatively on him. Yet now someone had sounded the alarm, and the work would likely be delayed yet again.

As he watched, French soldiers came spilling from the barracks block, scrambling to respond to the sound of the bell, clutching muskets and cramming on shakos.

Dubertrand strode from the window to the door and flung it open. The two men posted as guards outside stared at him in surprise. Mere youths, not even yet able to grow a proper moustache, Dubertrand thought, like most of the so-called garrison assigned to protect him and his work. Boys who until recently had been led by a cowardly incompetent, though Dubertrand could at least be pleased he had stripped Major d'Arcy of any vestiges of command.

'What is happening out there?' he demanded of them. They exchanged a nervous glance before one found his voice.

'Someone has sounded the alarm, sir.'

It took great restraint for Dubertrand not to scream at the idiot.

'Why?' he asked instead, voice like the acid in one of his chemical experiments.

'We don't know, sir,' the other one admitted.

'Then find out,' Dubertrand shouted. 'You! Go and get Captain Marcelle!'

He returned to his office and spent the next fifteen minutes alternating between pacing and glaring out of the window. He wanted desperately to get back to work but knew all too well that his mind would be unable to settle with so much discord, with such unknown variables plaguing it.

Finally, the soldier returned with Captain Marcelle. Less welcome was the fact that d'Arcy was with them.

'Why are you still here?' Dubertrand snapped at him. 'I thought I relieved you of command?'

'The major was attacked while leaving the fort early this morning, sir,' Marcelle said. 'He was assaulted by the labourers, and two men accompanying him were killed.'

'Not simple labourers, but partisans,' d'Arcy spoke up. 'They are one and the same. I fear your workforce is utterly infested, monsieur.'

'That is what all this fuss is about?' Dubertrand demanded. 'Are you not soldiers of France? Can you not keep this horde of flea-bitten Spanish peasantry in line? All that I ask is that they continue to produce, produce!'

Marcelle looked at d'Arcy, seemingly on the cusp of speaking out, but hesitant. Dubertrand decided he might have made a mistake in promoting the major's immediate subordinate in his place. Clearly the man was still loyal to d'Arcy, or did not understand the sharp, unquestioning efficiency that Dubertrand required from those carrying out his orders.

'What is it?' Dubertrand snapped, looking from one to the other. 'Answer me!'

'The major and his two guards were not alone when they were attacked,' Marcelle said reluctantly.

'I was transferring the prisoners,' d'Arcy spoke up. 'The partisans rescued them, and they are again at large within the fort.'

Dubertrand stared, hardly believing what he was hearing.

'Get out,' he said to Marcelle. The captain left without another word.

'Where were you transferring the prisoners?' Dubertrand demanded of d'Arcy as soon as the door was shut. 'And why? I ordered them to be shot.'

'I placed them in the casement cell yesterday evening, for the night,' d'Arcy said. 'Captain Marcelle intended to carry out your orders this morning. I went and retrieved them before he could do so. I was on my way to the gatehouse, to hand them into the custody of General Girard, but we were attacked on our way. The prisoners were taken. They are somewhere amongst the workhouses, hiding along with the partisans amongst the labourers.'

Dubertrand turned away, paced back behind his desk, rearranged several papers on it, then clenched his fists in an effort to stop them from shaking.

He had to remain in control. He had to stay logical, analytic. That was when he was at his best. Anything less was unworthy of him.

'Are you admitting to me that you allowed the prisoners to escape?' he asked d'Arcy, voice low and hard. 'The very men sent here to kill me?'

'I allowed nothing, monsieur,' d'Arcy said stiffly. 'I thought after the workers were detained yesterday, there would have been greater security in the workhouses—'

'You think I am an idiot, d'Arcy?' Dubertrand breathed. 'You could not make your intentions any more obvious. At worst, you are in league with these Englishmen. At best, you view them as a piece of good fortune, and hope that they kill me. Then you will not be demoted, and no further dishonour will be attached to your misbegotten name.'

'You know nothing of honour,' d'Arcy replied, the iron as evident in his voice now as it was in Dubertrand's. 'You order men to murder without a second thought, and you work your factory hands half to death to meet your damnable quotas. You are a symbol of how far we have fallen.'

Dubertrand rounded the table, shaking with fury.

'Do not pretend to understand my work. You could not comprehend it even if you tried. You are a product of the old ways, the ways that are dying, that our emperor is stamping out all over Europe. I am the new. I am the progress this world so desperately needs. The light of science will illuminate the right and the wrong alike. The age of reason has come, and it will not be stopped by the cowardice and meddling of lesser men like you!'

'There is no light in what you are doing in this place. There is no reason to your cruelty. I have seen what the army has done here in Spain. The atrocities it has committed. And because I would have no part in it, I am sent here, to serve a brute like you. Intelligence you may have, Dubertrand, the sort of intelligence that comes out of a book, but what use is your shining new world when it brings with it the same cruelties as the old? When you have a factory in every town, when villages are knocked down for chimney stacks and rivers turn rotten with waste, will you have finished constructing this new reality? This great machine that swallows men whole and burns their bones to ash?'

Dubertrand struck d'Arcy. It took him time to realise he had done so with the bust of Antoine-Laurent de Lavoisier, which he had snatched up from his desk without even realising it.

The major recoiled, blood on his brow.

The fury was still on Dubertrand. He hit him again, before he could recover, kicked him, knocked him to the floor. The major put up a hand to try and defend himself, stunned, his nose probably broken. But Dubertrand wouldn't stop. He had come too far for that.

At length, he became aware of figures in the open doorway. He finally ceased and looked up at them, discovering Captain Marcelle and the guards, staring, their faces white as the pages of one of his formula ledgers.

He was panting. There was blood, blood everywhere, on his hands and the front of his suit, on the floor rug, on Dubertrand's uniform, but most of all on the major's head, on his face. His barely recognisable face.

Dubertrand breathed out, slowly. He could control this. Fix it. He had to. He'd come too far.

He stood up, placed the bust back on his desk, then clutched his hands behind his back so they could not see the shaking.

'Major d'Arcy assaulted me,' he told Marcelle. 'He is a traitor to France, and his emperor. He has paid the price.'

'I don't think—' Marcelle began to say, but Dubertrand raised a finger sharply.

'Choose your next words very carefully, Captain. Am I not correct that the major removed the English prisoners from the gaol this morning without any authority other than his own?'

'Well, yes.'

'And that he was present when those prisoners rejoined the Spanish vagabonds lurking within these walls?'

'Yes, but—'

'You also witnessed Major d'Arcy attack me, did you not, immediately after I had laid out incontrovertible evidence that he was in league with the partisans, and the *rosbifs*.'

Dubertrand stared Marcelle down. Eventually, the captain dropped his gaze.

'Yes, Monsieur Dubertrand,' he said, his voice becoming quiet.

'Very good,' Dubertrand said brusquely, not wanting Marcelle to sense his relief. 'It is good to know, Captain, that you were not involved likewise in this treachery, and that there are still men in this garrison I can rely upon. Now, get this body out of my office, and take the rug with it. I want it replaced, or I'll catch a chill. And after that, I want a messenger sent to Girard. Tell him we are under attack! That we must have reinforcements, now! That I am betrayed at every turn, and my life is in mortal peril!'

Marcelle nodded, seemingly unable to speak, and hurried off, leaving the two pale-faced guards to heave d'Arcy out, dragging the major unceremoniously, partially wrapped up in the bloodied rug.

Dubertrand bowed his head when the door was shut, almost groaning with relief. It had been too close, all of it. But sometimes, action had to be taken for there to be reaction. He had done what needed to be done.

He saw that blood was running down Lavoisier's face and onto his papers, marking them with spots of deep red, spoiling them. Snarling, he knocked the bust off onto the floor.

Only then, at last, could he find enough peace of mind to get back to work.

Chapter Nineteen

Fort Josephine, Zaragoza, North-Eastern Spain,
October 28th, 1809

PLUNKET MARSHALLED HIS thoughts, and called together Mackintosh, Fraser and the partisans by the flickering light of the cellar's candles.

'The river is our best chance of getting out,' Fraser started to say, clearly misunderstanding Plunket's intentions. 'The gates and walls will be too heavily guarded.'

'I've told you before, we're not leaving until Dubertrand is dead,' Plunket said.

'The whole fort will be crawling with soldiers. Are you proposing fighting your way into the villa with a few dozen ill-armed partisans?' Fraser responded with a rare flash of exasperation.

'Ask Maria if the gunpowder is still being loaded onto the barges,' Plunket said. Reluctantly, Fraser did so.

'The workers have been ordered to continue the loading today, yes,' he translated in response. 'It will probably be done by tonight though.'

'Then Dubertrand will either be there, or overseeing it from the window of the villa,' Plunket said. 'I saw out of it when he took us into his office. I know which one it is.'

'And how close are you planning on getting to him?' Fraser said, gesturing at the firearms that had been removed from the barrels. 'These muskets are all smoothbore, and the French have your rifles!'

'Not all of them,' Plunket pointed out. 'But if what I'm planning is to go any further, I need to get back onto that church roof.'

MARIA WAS AS good as her word.

A tunnel had been dug from the wine cellar to the former basement of what the partisans claimed was now the fort's main cookhouse, similarly undiscovered by the French above. At the opposite end was another tunnel, this one freshly excavated and barely large enough for a man to fit through on his hands and knees.

Maria stated it led to the church crypt. After explaining what he intended to do, Plunket removed his sling so he could at least use his forearm, then followed her and two other partisans though the hole, with Mackintosh and Fraser tailing behind.

The tunnel was distressingly narrow, but Plunket forced himself on, on his knees, one hand and an elbow, trying not to think about the weight of earth pressing down all around, barely held at bay by the rudimentary struts the partisans had constructed.

'This is what I imagined the bowels of Hades would be like when I was a child,' Fraser murmured behind him.

'The bowels of what?' Plunket snapped, not looking back.

'Nothing,' Fraser said. 'Only the burden of a wasted education.'

'What, are you trying to say you regret being here?' Mackintosh spoke up from the back, his tone humorous.

'It's an honour to do my duty, for king and country,' Fraser said. 'Even when that involves grubbing through the dirt like a worm.'

'Well, I suppose some poor bastard's got to do it,' Plunket growled. 'The king-and-country part, I mean.'

Eventually the tunnel opened out. Maria offered her hand to Plunket as he emerged from the hole and helped him to his feet, a favour he passed on to Fraser and then Mackintosh. He would have laughed at their bedraggled, dirty appearances, if their current circumstances weren't so desperate.

The hole had been concealed behind a cracked old tomb, the wall next to it partially collapsed. Sunlight beaming in through a damaged door above illuminated the rest of the crypt, dusty and cold and dank.

Maria led them between the tombs and cobwebbed bone ossuaries, to a set of stairs at the far side of the grim chamber. At their top was a doorway that had been blocked off by fallen timbers, the wood charred and blackened by fire. The partisans began to dismantle it as silently as possible.

They passed through, and Plunket discovered they were in the main body of the church, or at least the bones of its carcass – much of the insides had been gutted. As Plunket had hoped, there were no French troops directly inside. Given they didn't know of the passages connecting the crypt to the outside, they had no reason to set guards within.

The group picked their way as quickly as they dared across the debris-choked nave, towards the door leading up into the tower. Maria muttered something as they reached it, and Fraser translated.

'She says there will probably be lookouts above us. She will deal with them.'

Plunket smiled and offered her a slight bow. 'Ladies first.'

Maria drew one of her knives from the pockets of her dress and, along with one of the other two partisans, slipped through the blackened hole that had once been the tower's ground-floor doorway. The rest waited in tense silence. Eventually they heard the sound of footsteps descending back down the stairs. Maria and her accomplice reappeared, her dress speckled with blood.

'*Ellas estan muertas,*' she said.

They climbed, up to the doorway that led out onto the edge of the roof, the very place they had been captured before. As soon as he emerged, Plunket saw the danger – there were French soldiers posted outside the front of the church, and patrolling the alleyways of the workhouse area beneath. None of them happened to glance up before he withdrew back inside.

'Stay here,' Plunket urged Fraser and the others inside the tower, trusting the lieutenant to pass his words on to Maria. 'The more of us there are out there, the greater the risk of discovery. I'll go alone.'

'But your hand,' Fraser started to whisper.

'I'll be fine,' Plunket growled. 'Tell her.'

After a short conversation with Maria, she seemed to acquiesce.

'We'll wait for you in the tower,' Fraser said. 'Godspeed.'

Plunket edged along the roof, forced to go painfully slowly to avoid disturbing any loose tiles. A pair of guards passed by along the alleyway beneath, talking in French, the tips of their fixed bayonets gleaming. He kept still until they had passed.

Eventually he reached the point opposite the stable roof, and the section containing the hatch leading down into the structure beneath. He remained there, poised, waiting to make sure the alleyway was clear and considering the odds of what he was doing. It was madness, he supposed. He was pursuing his orders beyond reasonable bounds, fuelled not simply by duty, but by his own stubbornness, his anger at being sent to this place by the likes of Simpson and, most of all, by the knowledge that if he turned back now, the deaths of Smith and Jones would have been in vain. They didn't deserve the ignominy of an unmarked mass grave with nothing gained. Their deaths – more akin to murder than honest killings in a true battle, Plunket thought – needed to be redressed. Blood for blood, the old way.

He wondered what the priest he had used to confess to would have said if he admitted to such things. If he had spoken of the shot he had taken in that sweltering steeple in Buenos Aires. Red blood, bright upon a white flag. Honour stained, ruined.

To hell with honour, and confession.

Plunket jumped.

The sound of his body impacting against the stable roof seemed loud enough to wake the dead. He scrabbled forward, and ended up hitting his injured hand, the sudden jab of pain forcing out a strangled cry. He managed to get out of sight of the street, then lay on his back, heart slamming, teeth clenched while he listened and tried to ignore the agony shooting up his right arm. He expected to hear shouts, the sounds of running feet, but there was nothing.

Eventually, the worst of the pain receded to a dull throb. He crept along the roof to the hatch and was relieved to find it unlocked. It creaked as he drew it back, forcing him to go slow. He peered into the darkness within, letting his eyes adjust, hunting for any sign of activity in the stable loft. There was movement further below, but nothing on the level directly beneath.

He climbed down the ladder, one-handed, silently cursing the groaning rungs with every breath, down into the loft. There, another pause, watching, waiting, listening, certain he was on the brink of being discovered.

He was certainly not alone. Besides the horses beneath him, shifting about in their stalls, there were people, difficult to discern between the loft's floorboards and the half-light. He heard voices, speaking Spanish – the stable hands, he presumed. No sign of soldiers within the building, though there were certainly some right outside.

He stepped carefully, wary of making the boards creak. He should have closed the hatch – anyone who looked up into the loft would see it was open, sunlight beaming in. Too late to go back now. Any delay would be an even greater risk.

As silently as possible, he began to dig in among the hay filling the back of the loft. He had concealed his rifle here more out of spite than a genuine belief he would be able to double back for it, simply determined that the French wouldn't take his Baker. Now, abruptly, finding it had become the only genuine hope of avenging Smith and Jones.

The hay was dense and matted but looked undisturbed. He dragged it apart one slow handful after another, being as quiet and possible, worried that dust and stray pieces of straw might be drifting down between the planks into the stable below.

If those tending the horses discovered him, would they alert the French? After Carlos's betrayal, he couldn't be sure.

It seemed to take a long time but, finally, his fingertips brushed against familiar, cold brass. Forcing himself not to rush, he unearthed the rifle's butt and then drew it out slowly, wary that, although he remembered leaving it on half cock, he might trigger an accidental discharge.

The weapon came free without incident. He cradled it in his elbow, made clumsy by the injury Dubertrand had inflicted.

Recovering the rifle was good news, but just as important was the fact he had left it patched and rammed. He could make another patch out of simple ripped cloth, but he didn't know if the varying calibres of the crude assortment of firearms the partisans had concealed beneath the fort would furnish any bullets that would match the Baker's

.62 bore. If it was going to come down to a single shot, he also preferred the finer powder he had primed it with but couldn't be sure it hadn't become damp or fouled in the day it had spent in the hay.

He quietly snapped open the hammer, peering down at the black powder grains in the pan, lightly probing them with a left-hand fingertip. They seemed dry, uncongealed. It was a risk using it, but repriming also might reduce the quality of the shot.

It would do for now. He closed the hammer and, checking it was still half cocked, slung it by its black leather sling across his back. Then, hardly daring to breathe, he climbed back up onto the roof.

More French were passing below. He heard the sound of hooves as well. Rising up just high enough to peer along the rooftop towards the fort's parade, he found himself looking at French cavalry, dragoons and more bastard lancers.

They must have come from the town. That meant Dubertrand had requested reinforcements and was receiving them. The odds against him were lengthening.

He made the jump and rejoined the others.

Chapter Twenty

Fort Josephine, Zaragoza, North-Eastern Spain, October 28th, 1809

THEY MADE IT back into the wine cellar without incident. There, Plunket finished composing his plan and laid it out for the others.

Only Fraser voiced any sort of objection.

'Shouldn't we wait?' he suggested. 'If what you said about the reinforcements is correct, the fort will be on the highest possible alert. In a few days it will probably be calmer, and therefore easier to move around. There seems to be no reason not to hold out down here for the time being.'

Previously, Plunket might have been suspicious that such a point came from a place of cowardice, but he had seen enough of the young officer in the past month to know that wasn't the case. He was simply eager, and people of his age and station were accustomed to thinking nothing of voicing their opinion.

'The gunpowder will be gone, likely by tonight,' Plunket told him. 'I'm sure the army back on the Guadiana would appreciate us stopping that shipment, but the most important thing is we have a better chance of rousing Dubertrand from his lair if we strike while the shipment is still being loaded. He clearly knows how important the powder is, and he's not the sort of man who responds well to being challenged. If we hit the gunpowder, he'll likely show himself. If we don't, there's every chance he'll simply remain at work in his office, and we won't be able to get a shot.'

Fraser accepted the point. Mackintosh, Maria and the partisans were already in agreement.

'You know that even if this works, it will come at a price, to you and your people,' he told Maria.

She delivered a long and impassioned reply, which Fraser steadily translated.

'She has already suffered, when the French burned her home and raped the sisters of her convent, and again when they corrupted her brother and killed her father. She says there is no price left that she would not be willing to pay. As for her people, they are the same, or they would not be here. They are ready to take vengeance for themselves, for their families and for their homes. Vengeance for Zaragoza.'

Plunket looked the woman in the eye and nodded, saying nothing more.

'She wishes to go and make the necessary preparations,' Fraser added.

'Yes,' Plunket said. 'We'll be ready when she is.'

MARIA DEPARTED FROM their hiding place first, back up into the workhouse. A messenger came down in her place about an hour later, saying that they should proceed.

'Ready?' Plunket asked Fraser. The youth had withdrawn for a while to the corner of the cellar, and when Plunket went to him, he was surprised to find he had removed his red coat in favour of a shabby tunic given to him by one of the partisans.

'If they take you like that—' Plunket began to say.

'I know,' Fraser spoke over him. 'But they were going to shoot us anyway, and I've no doubt if they apprehend us again, they'll finish the job. Besides, the longer we can blend in, the better. Red isn't exactly conducive to that, even with something over it.'

Plunket couldn't deny the truth of that. The lieutenant pulled on a black belt with a pouch stuffed with cartridges, then put on a battered, old cocked hat and hefted the musket he had been given.

'How do I look?' he asked with a sheepish smile.

'Like a Spanish rogue,' Plunket said, instinctively giving the lad a clap on the shoulder. For all the disdain he felt towards the privileged young men that served in the bottom rungs of the army's officer corps, at times it was difficult not to be infected by their youthful exuberance. He found himself second-guessing the instructions he had given, ones that would place Fraser in the midst of harm's way. But there was nothing that could be done about that. They were few enough as it was, and for there to be any hope of success, they would all have to share the danger.

Satisfied with Fraser's preparedness, he went over to Mackintosh. The other Scotsman seemed in a dourer mood than Plunket was accustomed to, sitting checking Plunket's rifle by the light of one of the candles.

'Is it ready?' Plunket asked.

'Seems to be,' Mackintosh said. 'Priming powder's fine, and the charge is still well sited in the breech.'

'You'll have to make the shot,' Plunket said. He'd handed his recovered rifle over to Mackintosh, knowing he would be no use with his hand broken. The other greenjacket had accepted the weapon, and the responsibility that came with it, only grudgingly.

'You've always complained about how much the lads talk about Cacabelos,' Plunket told him, trying to dredge him up out of his moroseness. 'Now's your chance to eclipse that. Shoot that bastard chemist, and I'm sure I'll never hear the end of it. It'll be "Plunket of the 95th" no more, but "Mackintosh of the 95th" every day.'

The good-natured badgering had little effect, except to draw the slenderest of smiles across Mackintosh's haggard face.

'That's assuming any of us live to tell the tale, even if the shot is made.'

That was true enough. Apart from Fraser's role, there was very little provision in the overall plan for escape. That was why Plunket had kept his rifleman's greens on, as had Mackintosh.

'Hopefully, if you put a bullet through Dubertrand, that French major will be left in charge,' Plunket pointed out. 'A man like that won't let us be shot.'

'You say that like we almost didn't get him murdered. Perhaps his view of us has changed.'

'Yes, but I was the one who saved his life. He owes me that much.'

It was a slender hope, and one that relied on killing Dubertrand in the first place, but it was better than nothing.

'For Jones, and Smith,' Plunket said, his own thoughts hardening as he contemplated their fallen friends. Mackintosh nodded, his expression now steely in the flickering half-light.

'Aye. Let's plug this wee hand-breaking chemist bastard.'

Chapter Twenty-One

Fort Josephine, Zaragoza, North-Eastern Spain, October 28th, 1809

FRASER WENT FIRST, up into the workhouse, accompanied by the other partisans.

He was afraid. His mouth felt dry, his palms felt clammy. As he climbed the stairs from the cellar, he found himself wondering what it might feel like to get shot.

He thrust such foolish thoughts from his mind. They would do no good. He needed to discover the mindset he had learned to fall back on when he had been a child, whenever he had been faced by undesirable circumstances. Doctor McGillvary's Greek and Latin lessons, or a midwinter Sunday sermon in the kirk, cold enough to make his whole body shiver. He'd always told himself that he didn't have a choice, that it was better to just get it over with, to not think about it and do it, and once it was done, he might even be glad of it.

This was no different, surely? He had to do his duty, anything else was unthinkable. No matter the price, it would be worth it.

Maria met him in the workhouse hallway with more of her compatriots. The small Spanish woman smiled at him, an expression that disarmed him.

'You look better without your red coat, Englishman,' she said in Spanish. He tried to find a proper response, but it came out garbled.

She laughed and introduced the others who would be joining him: six men and two women, all armed with blades and muskets from the partisans' hidden armoury.

'God speed you, Englishman,' she told him. He remembered abruptly that she had been a nun before the French had come to Zaragoza. An unlikely alliance, he found himself thinking, a Spanish nun and the middle son of a Scots Presbyterian minister. The thought made him smile back at her.

'Remember, straight for the jetty,' he told the eight assigned to him, accepting a cloak from one and doing his best to conceal his musket under it. 'We stop for nothing, understood?'

It was. He advanced to the doorway, opened it, and stepped out into the setting sun.

IN THE FORT'S main cookhouse, a woman calmly picked up the bowl of stew she had been given and threw it in the face of one of the soldiers overlooking the evening meal's distribution. Outraged, the Frenchman grabbed her by the arm. The Spaniard beside her then punched him in his slop-covered face, and the whole food hall descended into chaos.

It spread quickly, at it had been intended to. Some of the workers knew the plan, the rest were just happy to give hell back to their occupiers. Soon, a mob was forming outside the cookhouse's front doors and threatening to spill out onto the main parade.

Captain Marcelle ordered the dragoons newly arrived from the Zaragoza garrison to disperse the rioters. It was as they were forming up on the square that Maria struck.

She had taken three of the muskets from the cellar and now used one to shoot at the cavalry officer marshalling the dragoons from a workhouse window. The range across half of the parade was too great, but she hit the man's horse, and it bolted, throwing him in the process.

She felt a vicious sense of satisfaction, as she did any time she struck back against the invaders.

Now, there was no going back. She moved away from the window and told the two partisans who were with her in the upper room to take her place and keep up their fire for as long as they could. They snatched up the muskets and began shooting down at the dragoons, one loading while the other fired.

'Move between the windows, don't always use the same one,' she advised them, before hurrying downstairs and outside.

The mob before the cookhouse was continuing to swell, and a great cry went up from them as they heard the gunshots and saw the French officer fall.

The dragoons were disorganised, their commander still struggling to his feet, one NCO attempting to lead a part of the squadron towards the workhouse where the musket shots were coming from, while another shouted at a nearby officer on foot for the infantry to come up and support them.

Another minute and order would be restored: the infantry would flush the sharpshooters inside the workhouse, and the dragoons would canter forward and start cutting down and scattering the workers. But Maria wasn't going to give them a minute.

'Now is your time, brothers and sisters,' she shouted, drawing one of her knives. 'Hesitate now, and they will ride us down! Strike while they are disorganised! Follow me! For Zaragoza! For vengeance!'

With a scream ferocious enough to tear at her throat, she ran at the dragoons.

Roaring, the mob followed.

* * *

Fraser made it a little over halfway across the square before the French tried to stop him.

The far side had descended into utter carnage, as a mob of factory workers attacked the dragoons. French infantry were rushing to support the cavalry, with others charging towards the workhouses, where gunshots could be heard. There were still plenty more guards at the docks though, and it was one of those men who Fraser shot.

He had never fired at a man in anger before, let alone seen that man crumple before him. In the valley when the partisans had been ambushed, Plunket had shoved his fallen comrade's rifle into Fraser's hands, but he hadn't had the opportunity to shoot it. Likewise during their attempt to infiltrate the fort, he had grappled with a Frenchman, had known the flame and fury of combat, and in the heat of it would certainly have killed the man if he had been able to, but ultimately, he was the one who had ended up on the ground and a heartbeat away from death, had not the partisans saved them.

Though he would never admit it, certainly not to anyone in the army, the thought of taking another man's life had been something he had struggled with. As a child he had never been predisposed to violence, and it was his sense of duty and a desire for adventure that had caused him to seek a commission.

None of that mattered when he was confronted by an enemy soldier. The French at the wharf had noticed the sudden clutch of figures running past the riot, and several of the nearest moved to intercept them, shouting. One lowered his musket at Fraser, bayonet glinting as it caught the evening light.

In an instant, Fraser threw back his cloak and levelled his own musket, then fired. It was almost instinctive, a certainty that if he did not do so, he would be the one shot down.

The firearm kicked like a mule against his shoulder, and the smoke made his eyes sting, and then the Frenchman was down on the cobbles. Wounded or dead, Fraser did not know, and briefly, did not care. He ran over him, shouting incoherently, turning his musket to swing it like a club at the next soldier.

The battle was joined, and he was in the thick of it.

He led his little band of partisans in a charge, roaring, driving at the jetties. More muskets crashed, the Spaniards discharging point-blank into the nearest soldiers before setting about them with blades and commandeered work tools.

A savage excitement Fraser had never known gripped him, almost feral in its intensity, animalistic. He knocked a bayonet thrust to one side, the collision of the two barrels jarring his hands, and jabbed his own musket's butt up into his attacker's face, breaking teeth and toppling his shako. He followed up with a kick to the leg, bringing him down.

Directly ahead, workers on the jetties had turned on the last of the guards, while others were simply fleeing for the fort's gates. He experienced a surging sense of exultation as he saw they had reached their objective, and that the guards on the eastern flank of the wharf were too few to stop them.

'Stay together, and get to the boats,' he shouted to his compatriots, before realising he'd done so in English. He tried again in Spanish, and led a rush down the nearest jetty, shoes banging on the gangplanks.

Only then did he realise the problem. While there were still several half-full barges moored at the wharf, a number of the boats had already set off. They were visible further upriver, their crews rowing them away from the fort, the centre of each one stacked high with barrels of gunpowder.

'Bless me,' Fraser hissed under his breath, before waving the partisans into the nearest barge still moored up, explaining what they were going to do as they went.

The plan, up until that point, had been relatively simple, or at least his part in it had been. While Maria and the main body of the factory's workers provided a distraction, Fraser and his small force would break through to the docks and try to wreck as much of the gunpowder shipment as possible, either by scuttling the barges, or simply tossing barrels overboard. Concurrently, Plunket and Mackintosh would attempt to gain a vantage point – either the ruined church tower, or the roof of the factory itself – and hope that amidst the chaos, Dubertrand would show himself. A direct assault on the gunpowder made that more likely. The fort's parade was roughly a hundred yards square, so the range from the tower or the factory rooftop to the villa or the docks would be under two hundred – within rifle range.

Fraser was glad hunting down Dubertrand and taking the shot wasn't part of his responsibilities, even if storming the jetties seemed the more dangerous task. Now, though, he knew the job would only be half done if the barges that had already set off were allowed to escape. There was only one solution.

'Cast off,' he shouted to one of the partisans, who began to undo the rope anchoring the barge they had clambered into. Fraser seated himself in the bow, calling out to those left on shore.

'Do what you can to destroy the other barrels! Throw them in the river!'

In truth, given the fighting and the gunfire happening just yards from where a batch of the powder barrels were stacked, it seemed like it would take little to trigger a catastrophic detonation. Fraser had started his advance across the parade fearing that but now knew there was little he could do about it – his attention was all upriver. Plunket had given him a task, and he would not fail the rifleman.

'Oars out,' he called to his impromptu barge crew. 'Follow my count! Row!'

Chapter Twenty-Two

Fort Josephine, Zaragoza, North-Eastern Spain, October 28th, 1809

DUBERTRAND'S FOCUS WAS just returning when the swelling of voices followed by the unwelcome crack of a gunshot from outside shattered everything once more. He threw down his pen and stormed outside, ignoring his guards, who hesitated, then followed him onto the square.

The chemist emerged from the villa into a riot. Brawling Spaniards and Frenchmen were everywhere, the melee spilling from the parade's edge towards its centre. Dubertrand stared aghast as a dragoon just a dozen paces from the front door of the villa was dragged from his shrieking horse by a trio of grimy workers, who then set about beating him once he had fallen to the cobbles, his steed bolting in terror.

'Monsieur Dubertrand,' shouted a voice, intruding on his dismay. Captain Marcelle came pushing through to his side, sword unsheathed.

'Monsieur Dubertrand, please go back inside,' he said. 'My men and I cannot guarantee your safety out here!'

'What is happening?' Dubertrand exclaimed, a wave of his arm encompassing the carnage. 'They are rioting, Captain. Rioting!'

'It's the partisans, monsieur,' Marcelle said. 'And likely the British too. Please, go back inside.'

'Not until order is restored,' Dubertrand barked. 'This is an absolute disgrace, Marcelle!'

The captain began to reply, but Dubertrand refused to give him the opportunity.

'Have your men open fire on this peasant rabble,' he shouted. 'Then drive the survivors out of my fort at bayonet point! Show no mercy to any who resist! Open the eastern gate and sweep the scum out into the town! That old fool Girard can deal with any who survive!'

'As you wish,' Marcelle responded, seemingly with some effort, before he began to shout for one of his subalterns.

Dubertrand snapped at the two guards who had followed him out to stay close, and set off along the western edge of the square, towards the jetty.

The workers would be killed or driven out in short order. More labourers would then be found. What mattered was the gunpowder. If the latest shipment was delayed any further, or worse, destroyed, the consequences would be severe, and Dubertrand had no intention of being the one to pay them.

PLUNKET AND MACKINTOSH took the passageway back into the church's crypt.

Plunket had armed himself with a pair of Spanish pistols, loaded and stuffed into his belt. They were big, clumsy weapons, but they were the only ones suitable given his injury.

They climbed warily up into the musty crypt, the riflemen alone – all the partisans had gone to play their part. Maria had promised Plunket that she would stir up a storm for him, and it sounded as though it was about to break. He could hear a swelling roar rising from above, the sounds of an outraged mob. With it came the telltale crack of musket fire, one or two shots at first, but rapidly beginning to rise in intensity.

Men and women would be dying soon, Plunket thought, if they weren't already; dying in order that the two riflemen might get one moment, enough for a single, clear shot. He tried not to think about that as he headed for the stairs up into the church.

The intention was to use the structure's tower as a vantage point, but Plunket spotted as soon as he edged out into the ruined nave that there would be no hope of that. There was gunfire already ringing out from the tower, accompanied by shouts, echoing down the stairwell. The voices were speaking French – Plunket assumed some quick-thinking officer or sergeant had noticed the tower could act as a strongpoint and had occupied it when Maria's riot had got underway. He had feared something like that might happen and had discussed secondary options with Mackintosh.

'We head for the factory instead,' he told the Scot. The building's roof was even taller than the church tower and dominated the whole southern side of the fort. It was accessible by an open wooden stairway on either flank and would put them closer to the villa than the church would too. Plunket had only favoured the church because of the underground passageway providing an easy access point – to reach the factory, they would now have to traverse the warren of workhouses and outbuildings, and there was a possibility the French would have deployed extra forces to protect the vital structure from the mob.

They slipped out of the side door at the end of the transept, finding themselves in an alleyway between the church and the cookhouse. It was empty, though the sounds of rioting were even nearer, and a clutch of workers ran past the end of the alley without noticing them.

'This way,' Plunket muttered, leading Mackintosh in the other direction. Maria had drawn out a rough map of the fort interior and given it to him before leaving, and he had done his best to memorise it.

The alley intersected with another, leading around the rear of the cookhouse. Plunket paused before entering it. On impulse, he dragged one of the pistols from his belt. He had put his right arm back in its sling, and used his bound forearm to cock the flint, the heavy tension of the weapon's spring engaging combined with that familiar click at least offering a sense of security.

The narrow lane was filled with barrels and stinking food waste from the kitchens, and it was only as Plunket passed through it that he noticed that two men were sheltering there, behind a set of empty crates. They raised their hands hastily as Plunket jerked his pistol in their direction.

'*Español, señor,*' one stammered. They were wearing civilian clothing, as well as grubby aprons. Garrison cooks, Plunket assumed, probably sheltering from the riot that had broken out during the evening meal. He wondered how loyal they were to their paymasters, but decided to leave them alone, advancing warily past them without a word.

On the other side of the cookhouse, the alley opened out into the street that ran alongside the factory building. It towered above them now, a red-bricked industrial monolith, its four chimney stacks still churning filthy smog out into the evening air.

Plunket could see the stairway that provided access to the roof up the building's flank, but he also discovered a troop of French cavalry, with more infantry, stationed seemingly in reserve next to it. He ducked back hastily into the alleyway's cover, then waited to make sure he hadn't been spotted.

'Round the back,' he told Mackintosh. 'There's frogs everywhere.'

They doubled back along the cookhouse lane. The two Spaniards had fled. They carried on to the first alley by the church, then turned left instead of right, towards the fort's south-eastern bastion.

Plunket knew they didn't have much time. If the riot got out of hand, the French would respond with full force. It could quickly turn into a massacre, one that likely wouldn't take long to complete. While unrestrained killing by the garrison might help the plan to draw Dubertrand out – Plunket could imagine the deranged chemist would enjoy overseeing such a thing – he didn't wish to bring slaughter down on the ordinary factory workers. He had enough deaths on his conscience already.

Their new route took them along the actual base of the fort's wall. To Plunket's relief the earthen fortification was sparsely guarded, the garrison's efforts focused inward and not anticipating any threat from Zaragoza or beyond. The two riflemen made it into the shadow of the walls and passed along and under the gaze of the French there, intending to circle around to the lane that ran between the factory and the fort's southernmost bastion.

That was where their luck ran out.

They were just rounding onto the factory's corner when Plunket noticed that they weren't alone. There were French infantry stationed behind the lancers next to the factory's side stairs, but their attention was all in the opposite direction, towards the fighting happening in the square. All except one man, who had seemingly been given permission to fall out of the ranks to take a piss in the back alley.

The man was buttoning his breeches back up and glanced up just as Plunket and Mackintosh rounded the corner into the lane. They simply stared at one another. Then, the man snatched his musket from his shoulder and shouted.

'*Alarme! Ils sont là!*'

Plunket swore and shoved Mackintosh back. He briefly considered shooting the man and rushing the stairs, hoping to gain them in the confusion before they were cut off. He knew that would all be in vain – even if they made it to the stairs before the French, its open sides would mean they would make clear targets for a dozen or more muskets just yards away.

'Back to the church, sharpish,' he told Mackintosh, as he heard more shouts from the direction of the factory, and the noise of running feet.

Then came a far worse sound. Hooves on the cobbles.

It wasn't only the infantry in pursuit. He snatched a glance back and saw two lancers cantering into the alley after them.

Plunket and Mackintosh ran for their lives, back along the lane beneath the wall. The nightmarish, rhythmic clatter of steel-shod hooves grew rapidly louder, and with a sickening feeling Plunket realised they weren't going to make it past the next corner.

That left only one thing to do.

'Keep going,' he shouted to Mackintosh. Then he stopped, turned, raised his pistol, and fired.

Chapter Twenty-Three

Fort Josephine, Zaragoza, North-Eastern Spain, October 28th, 1809

FRASER'S BARGE GAINED quickly on the boats that had already left the fort. The partisans put in a ferocious effort on the oars and, more importantly, they were doing so unencumbered by the heavy barrels the other transports were moving upriver.

Fraser reloaded his commandeered musket as they gained on the nearest one, priming and then ramming home powder and ball. The pursuit had given time for the fiercest aspects of the rush of combat to dissipate, and he found his hands shaking as he worked the weapon. He thought again of how the Frenchman had poised his weapon at him on the jetty – would he have fired, if Fraser hadn't shot first?

He had no doubt the moment would hang over him but now was not the time to give it any thought. There were two French soldiers on the barge they were gaining on, guards set to see the precious powder safe to Marshal Soult's army, and one of them fired his own musket as the gap narrowed.

Fraser heard the ball slap past his head, the near miss making him flinch. His anger flared, and without thinking he brought his Spanish gun up to his shoulder and fired back.

Even as he felt the heat of the pan's flare and the kick of the butt, he understood his mistake. He experienced a heartbeat's horror, followed by the hope that he had missed.

The detonation put paid to that.

The barge ahead of them exploded. One instant it was there, and the next a wall of flame and smoke and timber debris was roaring outwards in its place.

Fraser's vengeful shot had hit the powder barrels. They had been packed in too high, stacked above the gunwales. The force of the blast knocked Fraser back into the oarsmen and kicked up a wave of water that threatened to capsize them.

He managed to right himself at about the same time as the boat, his face stinging from the heat of the blast. He stared aghast, ears ringing, burning planks of wood raining down around them. Choking smoke had engulfed them, but even without its pall it was clear the other barge was simply gone.

'Don't do that again, Englishman, or you might blow us all up,' one of the Spaniards warned. Fraser swallowed hard, feeling momentarily horrified at what he had done, but then the partisan was snapping at his fellows to start rowing again, and determination gripped Fraser once more.

'The other barges won't resist us after seeing that,' he pointed out. 'Let's get after them!'

PLUNKET'S PISTOL SHOT was a poor one, hurried, but the range was too short for him to miss. The ball clipped the first lancer's shoulder, making him cry out in pain and drop his weapon. He was almost on top of Plunket, and the rifleman reversed the pistol and swung its butt at the horse, snarling, knowing there was no time to reload.

The animal, already spooked by the weapon's discharge in its face, shrieked and reared, throwing its injured rider from the saddle before half twisting away. In the narrowness of the lane, the second lancer behind couldn't get past, and the two horses collided, knocking both down in a tangle of thrashing limbs and bodies.

Plunket threw himself back, narrowly avoiding one kicking hoof, and turned away to race after Mackintosh. To his credit the Scotsman had done as Plunket had instructed and had kept going, disappearing into the church alley. Plunket followed, discarding the empty pistol and dragging the second from his belt as he went.

He saw Mackintosh ahead of him, diving back into the cookhouse alley rather than carrying on to the church's side entrance. He saw why almost in the same instant. French infantry had appeared at the far end, presumably part of the factory detachment sent to cut them off. They were closer to the church entrance than he was, and several paused to fire, musket balls slashing past.

Plunket had no choice other than to run into the gunfire and race them to the cookhouse alley. Knowing better than to hesitate, he dashed forward. To the French it might briefly appear as though the lone rifleman was charging them, and their surprise bought just enough time for him to gain the alleyway, another salvo of shots tearing into the junction where he had been seconds before.

He knew the far end of the cookhouse lane would only end up taking them back to the factory, and presumably more French troops, but there had been a back entrance into the building that likely led to the kitchens. They could go through the cookhouse and out of the front, into the square. That would at least take them away from the trap the workhouse area was becoming, and they could reassess, perhaps temporarily get back down into the safety of the cellar network.

Then Plunket realised that they wouldn't be doing any of that.

Mackintosh was still ahead, almost halfway along the lane, but he wasn't alone. Another lancer had been sent down from the opposite direction. Mackintosh had impeded the man's charge by tossing the empty crates along the cookhouse's back wall into his path, causing the horse to shy. He swung over them with his rifle clubbed, going for the mount rather than the man, striking with the age-old infantryman's intention to disable the rider by unsettling or injuring his horse.

It almost worked. As had happened with Plunket, the lancer was unable to manoeuvre in the narrow lane, and Mackintosh was now inside the guard of his weapon – the long lance, so adept at spearing through infantry at full tilt, suddenly became cumbersome and unwieldy when the target was able to get in close.

Mackintosh was able to haul the lancer from his saddle as Plunket ran to join the fight. The horse bolted, knocking Mackintosh to one side before he could strike the sprawling lancer, crates splintering beneath the beast's hooves. Plunket had to throw himself hard against the alley's side to avoid being knocked over as well. By the time it was past him, the lancer was up on his feet, his long weapon still in hand.

'Shoot him,' Plunket shouted, even though he knew why Mackintosh didn't. His Baker rifle's charge was the last patched ammunition they had, the one remaining shot whose accuracy could be relied on. It was meant for Dubertrand.

Now, the advantage was back with the Frenchman. He threw himself into a stab, both hands gripping his weapon's haft. Plunket levelled his second pistol, but Mackintosh was between him and the target.

The lancer ran the rifleman through.

Plunket roared and lunged past Mackintosh as he fell, the Frenchman yanking his weapon free. He slammed the butt of his pistol against the lancer's face, kicked him, got him down in the dirt. In his fury, he dropped the pistol but managed to snatch the lance up. It had a blunted metal tip on its reverse end and, unable to easily turn the upper spike downwards, Plunket instead slammed the base through the man's breast, scraping it off ribs before puncturing heart and lungs, pinning the man to the refuse-littered filth of the cookhouse alley floor. The Frenchman convulsed with a cry, then went still.

'Damn it all to hell,' Plunket hissed as he abandoned the weapon and knelt hastily beside Mackintosh, clutching him. The Scotsman tried to speak, spitting dark blood as he did so.

'Just get the bastard,' he snarled, teeth red. 'Whatever it takes.'

Plunket nodded, not trusting himself to speak. He kept a grip on his friend for longer than he knew he should, until the other rifleman's eyes had lost their focus, and the pain-stricken tension had left his body.

A shout came from the far end of the alleyway. French infantry, crowding in. One raised his musket and fired, the lead ball punching a splinter from the cookhouse wall just above Plunket's head.

There were more coming from the other direction as well, cutting him off.

He let go of Mackintosh and picked up his rifle, slinging it before grabbing the pistol as well. The urge to stay and fight gripped him, to stand and kill the bastards, to take as many as he could before bayonets and clubbed muskets sent him to rejoin his friends.

But then it would all have been for nothing.

He rose and threw himself against the back door of the cookhouse, slamming through it and out of the alleyway.

Chapter Twenty-Four

Fort Josephine, Zaragoza, North-Eastern Spain,
October 28th, 1809

PLUNKET FOUND THE cookhouse kitchens and main hall deserted, tables overturned and plates and bowls spilled across the floor. The riot that had first started there had long swept out into the square.

He paused to heave one of the tables in the hall across the kitchen doorway before running for the front entrance, hearing the pounding of fists and musket butts on the timber behind him. He carried on, through the front doors and out into the square, and found himself in the midst of a scene of chaos.

It was a riot no more, but an outright battle between the workers and partisans, and the French garrison. He saw Spaniards dragging a dragoon from his mount and beating him with work tools. Further left, a French officer was leading a dozen men as they broke into one of the workhouses, presumably intent on getting at the partisan marksmen who were firing into the square from one of the upper storey windows.

A trumpet shrilled, and a fresh squadron of lancers came cantering from the direction of the villa across the square, charging into the melee with lances lowered.

'*Saltamontes!*'

The shout came from nearby, and Plunket found Maria pushing her way through the press of bodies. She had a knife in each hand, and her dress was even bloodier than before.

'*¿Por qué estás aquí? ¡El químico parece ir a los muelles!*' she barked, but Plunket couldn't understand her. She waved one of her knives in the direction of the docks and shouted another word that Plunket did recognise.

'*Francés! Francés!*'

She or her partisans must have seen Dubertrand moving towards the river. It was what they had hoped. The gunpowder shipments were the very reason for the fort's existence, and ensuring they were protected during a riot would surely be the chemist's foremost priority.

Of course, without a perch and with one hand broken, using the rifle to kill him would be next to impossible. At least he still had one loaded pistol. He would just have to get close.

'Thank you,' he shouted to Maria, and set off through the square.

THE FRENCH DROVE the rioters back. The lancers around the factory counterattacked, and Marcelle's infantry were able to find the order they needed to reform and drive the mob along the wider roadway leading to the eastern gate. Men and women were shot, bayoneted and trampled. It became a massacre, rather than a battle.

Marcelle ordered the eastern gate to be thrown open. The factory workers were driven out through it and into the town.

Maria had not planned on going with them. She was in a frenzy, a knife in each hand, forearms drenched with blood almost up to her elbows. She had been like an elemental force in the midst of the chaos, alternating between killing and directing the efforts of the mob. And in the middle of it all she had been able to forget, for a time, forget the pain and the frustration and the feelings of helplessness that had plagued her ever since Zaragoza had been sacked, and her world had been ravaged and burned down.

For a brief time, she became vengeance incarnate and rejoiced in it.

It had almost looked as though the rioters might actually win, that Fort Josephine's garrison could find itself completely overrun. But then, on Dubertrand's urging, the French had cast aside all restraint and committed their reserves. For all her fury, for all her wrathful effort, Maria couldn't stop the Spanish from being driven towards the gatehouse.

'We need to get out,' Enrico, her cousin, shouted over the tumult, snatching her shoulder and halting her before she could throw herself onto the levelled bayonets of a wall of oncoming French infantry.

'The grasshopper still hasn't taken his shot yet,' Maria snapped back at him.

'And you dying here won't change that,' Enrico exclaimed. 'If the English have not done what they came here to do by now, they never will!'

He dragged her backwards, into the shadow of the gatehouse, in amongst the press of bodies cramming through it and spilling out into the streets of Zaragoza.

'Let them go,' Marcelle shouted at his men, watching as the remains of the rebellious workforce scrambled and shoved their way out through the gate, leaving the dead and the dying scattered thickly in their wake.

'Sir, we have them trapped,' one of his subalterns said. 'We can close the gate and cut them all down!'

'You'll do no such thing,' Marcelle snapped at the young officer. There were partisans amidst the mob, but he wouldn't open fire into beaten, fleeing men and women on the pretext that the enemy were hiding among them. Besides, letting them pour out through the open gate would clear the fort quicker than attempting to kill them all.

He wondered, if Dubertrand had ordered him to do just that, whether he would have had the strength to refuse him, the strength he had failed to show when it had come to supporting Major d'Arcy. He thought again about the murder he had witnessed, and how he had meekly submitted to his commander's killer in its aftermath. It was a shame he knew he would never blot out.

'Close the gate behind them,' he ordered the subaltern firmly. 'And get me a courier. I want word sent to General Girard. The streets are going to be busy tonight.'

At least seizing fleeing partisans and ensuring the riot didn't spread into Zaragoza would be someone else's problem, Marcelle thought.

For now, all that mattered was that the fighting was over. Fort Josephine was secure.

Chapter Twenty-Five

Fort Josephine, Zaragoza, North-Eastern Spain, October 28th, 1809

PLUNKET MADE FOR the docks as the sun began to set, casting bloody hues over the slaughter yard of the fort's interior.

He had tried to skirt the carnage in the square, but the tide of bodies had carried him east, and he was forced to break free and return to the workhouse alleys as the French gained ground. From there, he worked his way along the base of the northern walls, overlooking the river and finally reached the entrance to the jetties.

Once there, he discovered he was too late.

The fighting at the river was over. There were French infantry and cavalry everywhere, and the workers who had rebelled were either all dead or had jumped into the river and were swimming desperately for the far bank. The sounds of fighting elsewhere had ceased as well, only the occasional musket shot marking where the French were clearing the last of the workhouses and alleyways.

Worst of all, there was no sign of Fraser or his detachment of partisans. Dozens of barrels were still stacked along two of the three jetties, with more waiting in the covered way leading back behind the villa to the factory. The French had already started loading the last moored barges, the soldiers now transporting the cargo themselves, intent on getting them away without further delay.

Plunket knew it was hopeless. There was gunfire from above him, from the bastions guarding the river entrance, lead balls cracking into the cobbles at his feet. More came from behind, from a detachment of infantry who had just appeared from clearing the workhouses. They began to run after Plunket, bayonets lowered.

With nowhere else to go, he ran for the nearest jetty. There were no soldiers on it, probably because it was the only one that had already been fully cleared of barrels. A single Frenchman charged him from the neighbouring jetty, so he shot him with his second pistol, causing the man to tumble into the river.

He knew he had wasted the bullet, but it hardly mattered anymore.

The Ebro lay before him, its dark waters running cold and quick. He could jump, strike out, and hope that any of the French firing at him from the jetties would miss their mark. The thought of such effort, and what lay beyond – trying to evade the enemy's patrols while making his way back through an alien country during winter – was more than he could bear.

So he stood, staring grimly out over the river, until a voice called out behind him.

'Going so soon, *rosbif*?'

He turned back to face the fort. French soldiers were storming down the jetty towards him, the gangplanks shivering under their feet. Behind them stalked a figure in dark clothes, a shadow in the midst of the brilliant red and gold of the setting sun – Dubertrand.

Without thinking, Plunket brought the rifle from his shoulder and cocked it, the barrel resting against his slung-bound right forearm.

The French infantry halted, levelling their muskets, barely a dozen yards away. Dubertrand, too, had stopped, still far back, lingering at the jetty's entrance.

'I thought you came to kill me, yet here I am, still breathing,' the chemist called out, his tone razor sharp, bleeding triumph. 'Was that what all this was about? All this slaughter and death? What a waste!'

Plunket assessed the range. Under fifty yards. An easy shot, if one hand wasn't broken and the target wasn't almost wholly obscured by the French soldiers between them. Those factors combined made it impossible.

'How do your men feel, fighting and dying for a lunatic who hides behind them?' Plunket demanded, glaring past the soldiers at Dubertrand. The chemist laughed.

'You think I am as stupid as you are, *caporal?* That I'm going to let you goad me into approaching you, just so you can shoot me down? What kind of fool do you think I am?'

'The worst kind, one who's convinced of the greatness of his own knowledge. You're a child, Dubertrand. An angry child who tells everyone he's a genius and throws fits of rage when they don't believe him.'

That at least drew a moment's hesitation, anger that Dubertrand had to master. But the Frenchman made no move to approach, and Plunket knew he wouldn't.

'You've wasted enough of my time, *rosbif*,' Dubertrand snapped. 'Time to die.'

Plunket was beaten, and he knew it.

He thought about Smith, impaled by a lance as he ran, and Jones, shot down by a traitor, and Mackintosh. He remembered the Scotsman's last words. He thought about that freezing cold day outside Cacabelos, and that burning hot cauldron of death in Buenos Aires.

He'd never been very good at accepting defeat.

Baker rifle still braced against his forearm, he turned to point it towards the neighbouring jetty and, in the last of the day's dying light, pulled the trigger.

The ball whipped across the water and the barge moored there; it punched through the timber of one of the large stacks of barrels still waiting on the gangplanks.

Plunket's cry of pain as the recoil jarred his broken hand was lost in the ear-splitting thunder of the barrels detonating. The lead ball, hot from the fire of the rifle's discharge, touched off the volatile black powder within, and an inferno roared out across the jetty.

That initial explosion was nothing compared to what came after. The blast touched off the barrels still in the covered way, which channelled the fire, creating a chain reaction that Dubertrand might have been proud of, had he not been screaming with horror.

The explosions reached the factory, and that was when the true detonation occurred. The vast stocks of chemicals went off in a blinding flash.

The explosion was apocalyptic. It blew the factory apart, sent its four smokestacks crashing down, turned the workhouses, stables and outhouses to matchwood, levelled Fort Josephine's walls on the southern, eastern and western sides, and demolished Dubertrand's villa. Only the church tower was left standing, barely, teetering amidst the wasteland of smoke and fire, churned earth and blackened debris.

Dubertrand and the men around him were incinerated amidst the secondary explosions that blasted the dock to pieces.

Plunket was not among them. The shockwave from the initial explosion had knocked him backwards, into the river. The cold water was a shock, and it churned around him with the battering fury of the main detonation, and then the hail of debris that followed, dragging him under.

He choked and struggled, before a sudden calmness gripped him, as cold as the river itself.

He welcomed death. It was long overdue. He should have perished before, amidst the heat and the flying metal atop that church spire in Buenos Aires, or in the ice and snow of Galicia. It was his friends who had saved him before, and now they were all gone. Perhaps it was time he joined them.

In those dark depths he knew peace, and silence, while above him the fire raged.

Then he broke the surface. He gasped, dragging air into lungs, coughing first on water and then on ash. He lashed out instinctively, his body unable to simply accept a watery grave. His eyes stung, the world reduced to smoke and falling debris and the two deadly opposites of fire and water.

His sling had come away and his right hand was in agony, but he still had his rifle, its leather strap snagged around his right elbow. It threatened to drag him down, but he kicked out, lunging for a curved length of wood bobbing in the water beside him, the shattered remains of one of the powder barrels.

He managed to grasp it, then feared it wouldn't be able to support him as he momentarily went under again, but the driftwood rediscovered its buoyancy, and he clung on, flinching from the pain in his hand and from the unidentifiable, burning debris still falling all around.

The jetties and their boats and barrels were simply gone, and it seemed as though much of Fort Josephine beyond it was as well. A blazing wall of flames was rising up from the ruined timber of the docks, and smoke and ash shrouded everything. There was no sign of Dubertrand – no sign of any survivors at all. A single shot had reduced the factory and its surrounds to a burning wasteland.

Plunket simply drifted for a while, exhausted, drained of any resolve to act. The smoke began to settle more thickly, making him cough and splutter once more. He tried to kick out for the shore opposite the fort but couldn't find the strength to do so. He could barely hold on.

Slowly, he became aware of a shape amidst the shroud of destruction, coalescing in the twilight further upriver.

It was too large to be a piece of debris, and as it drew nearer Plunket realised it was one of the gunpowder barges. It seemed impossible that any might have survived the destruction of the jetties – Plunket could only assume it had come down from upriver.

He tried to hail it, his voice weak. The starboard oars were raised, and it slid up alongside, a figure leaning over the prow to peer down at him.

'Bless me,' exclaimed a voice. Plunket found himself looking up into the powder-blackened face of Lieutenant Fraser.

Hands grasped at him, and he let go of the driftwood as he was hauled up over the gunwales, groaning with pain as the rough motion jarred his hand. He managed to sit up, facing Fraser, who was still perched in the prow.

'I told them,' the subaltern said excitedly, clutching the sopping green cloth of Plunket's right arm and leaning in as he spoke over the roar of the flames, still perilously close. 'I told them if there were any survivors, you'd be among them!'

A Spaniard threw a cloak over Plunket's shoulders. He couldn't find any words to reply, so simply sat, shivering.

'Mackintosh…' Fraser began to ask. Plunket shook his head, and the lieutenant became silent, before one of the partisans posed him a question.

'He wants to know if we should row upriver, or down,' Fraser translated.

'Doesn't matter,' Plunket grunted. Fraser's expression very much implied that it did, but eventually he gave his own orders to his crew. The Spanish started to heave on their oars again, the barge's prow bumping aside burning wreckage as it made its way along the debris-choked river.

'We got all of them,' Fraser reported. 'The barges, I mean. We had to commandeer this one and row it upriver to catch the first that had left. We made the crews throw the barrels into the river. Every last one of them. That's them ruined.'

'Good,' Plunket managed to say. It was done then. It hadn't all been in vain.

'Was... was that you?' Fraser asked him after a short silence, not having to state just what he was referring to. The burning carcass of Fort Josephine was beginning to recede now, a wall of smoke lit by a core of raging fire, the plumes from its chimney stacks now replaced by a vast black thunderhead that melded with the encroaching darkness of the night. Ash had started to fall across the river, a deathly snowfall in the gathering gloom.

'Yes, it was,' Plunket admitted eventually. 'A single shot.'

Epilogue

Lisbon, Portugal,
December 21st, 1809

'SEND THEM IN,' the Duke of Wellington growled.

An aide opened the door, and two figures stepped into the drawing room, halting at attention in front of the desk Wellington had occupied for the afternoon. The one on the left saluted – the one on the right made no motion, his right hand bandaged and the arm in a sling.

Wellington permitted the irregularity.

'Stand easy, gentlemen,' he said, putting down the pen he had been writing with and leaning back in his chair to survey them both. Lieutenant Fraser, no longer in his smart red uniform, but looking for all the world like some Spanish vagabond, and Corporal Plunket, even more raggedy than when the duke had last seen him. He supposed that couldn't be helped.

'Welcome back,' he said.

Neither replied, the only sound the steady ticking of the large clock standing in one corner of the ornately furnished room. The house belonged to one of Britain's diplomatic attachés in Portugal, but Wellington was using it for the afternoon to catch up on correspondence and conduct meetings and interviews. The main body of the army was still in Spain, but plans were afoot for a withdrawal into Portugal, and he was in Lisbon frequently anyway – it was the main line of communication back to Britain, and there had recently been a great deal of work to oversee outside the Portuguese capital, putting into action a plan he had spent some months formulating.

That particular morning had been dedicated to another meeting with Mister Simpson, and the newly returned survivors of the Zaragoza operation. Simpson himself was standing in his usual place, off to one side, as was Lieutenant Colonel Robertson. He had already informed Wellington of the rough particulars of what had happened at Zaragoza. By some wild, near-inconceivable exertion, not only had the chemist Dubertrand been killed, but the entire Leclerc factory and its base of operations had been destroyed. Simpson's networks had informed him that Marshal Soult was greatly perturbed, and that partisan operations across Iberia were now escalating, buoyed by the daring success. There were even rumours that Bonaparte himself was furious, and that Soult was soon to be replaced by another of the emperor's generals.

It had all gone far better than Wellington had dared hope.

'You have the army's thanks, as well as mine,' he told Fraser and Plunket. 'By the sound of it, it was a damned fine service you rendered. I'd hear more of it from you now, first hand.'

Lieutenant Fraser supplied a succinct report of what had happened, including how they had eventually made their way back to the army. Following Fort Josephine's destruction, they had taken the barge downriver before abandoning it on the south bank of the Ebro. After that, the partisans had made contact with more of their kind, including Maria, who had escaped Zaragoza in the midst of an attempted lockdown on the orders of the local commander, General Girard. A month and a half had then been spent evading capture, first making for the Costa Dorada, where they had tried and failed to reach one of the Royal Navy's Mediterranean squadrons, then south, eventually rejoining the British army as it prepared to follow its commander in a strategic winter withdrawal into Portugal.

'I can submit this all in writing as well, sir, if you require,' Fraser offered.

'Perhaps best if you do not, Mister Fraser,' Wellington cautioned him. 'Such work rarely benefits from a trail of papers. I fear you must surrender the possibility of a place in the future histories of this war, at least on this occasion.'

'I understand,' Fraser said. 'As long as I have done my duty to your satisfaction.'

'You have,' Wellington allowed. 'And there should be some reward. Promotion for both of you, certainly. I'll see it done.'

'With respect, sir, there's just one thing I would like,' Plunket spoke up, to Wellington's surprise. 'A pardon.'

'For what?'

'Striking a superior officer, sir.'

'A superior officer? Who? When was this?'

Plunket didn't reply but instead turned towards Simpson. Without further warning, he punched the spymaster, a left hook that connected with a heavy thump against the man's flabby jaw.

Simpson staggered, banging into the ticking clock and almost knocking it over. He clutched his face, staring at Plunket in abject shock, an expression that swiftly changed to ruddy, outraged anger.

Plunket just glared back at him, before turning to Wellington.

'Just now, sir.'

Wellington could not stop himself from letting out a short bark of laughter.

'That was for my men,' Plunket said, sparing Simpson another glance, as though daring him to complain. 'Riflemen Smith, Jones and Mackintosh. They gave their lives for your little scheme. They were better men than me, and far better men than you, and if there was any justice in the world, they'd be the ones standing here, and not me.'

'We owe them a debt we cannot repay, is that not so, Mister Simpson?' Wellington demanded, looking hard at the spymaster. Simpson's furious expression bled away, replaced by that sly, knowing look, the mask he wore so carefully and which Plunket had succeeded, however briefly, in knocking off.

'Of course, Your Grace,' he said, realising he had no recourse to avenge the blow. Wellington hoped that, deep down, the spymaster perhaps even accepted that he had deserved it.

'I wish to speak freely,' Plunket said, addressing Wellington. 'To Lieutenant Colonel Robertson.'

'Go on,' Wellington said guardedly. 'But you should know I won't tolerate any more insubordination from you, Corporal Plunket. Even heroes must still obey the king's regulations.'

'Understood, sir,' Plunket said, looking at Robertson. The Rifles officer stood before Plunket unflinchingly – Wellington doubted he would accept a blow the way Simpson had.

'I want to apologise, sir,' Plunket said to him. 'I mean formally apologise, for what happened before. In Buenos Aires. I heard you order us not to fire. I shouldn't have shot that Spaniard. I know what happened afterwards was my fault. All the lads that were killed…' He trailed off, seemingly lost for words.

'You were lucky not to end up counted among the dead that day, Plunket,' Robertson said gravely.

'I know, sir. Sometimes I wish I had. I know apologising won't make any difference, but I wanted you to know I don't take any of it lightly. I'm a sinner, sir. All I can do is repent.'

'Aren't we all?' Robertson said, a little more softly this time.

Wellington grimaced.

'A bad business, gentlemen. But it's all in the past, for better or for worse. And I need you in the present. The new year is almost upon us, and I suspect what awaits us when the weather turns will make the last few campaigns look like a picnic. The French will be upon us, and their intent will be to claim all of Iberia.'

He drew a map across the desk and tapped a finger in the vicinity of Lisbon.

'You may have noticed on your ride here, but work is now underway to erect a defensive string of fortifications around the capital. They're sited here, at Torres Vedras, but when the lines are complete, they'll extend all across the hills overlooking the town. If the worst should happen, and the French should drive us from the Spanish border and through Portugal, I intend to retreat here and make my stand.'

'Hopefully it won't come to that, sir,' Fraser said.

'Whether it does or not, it'll be the devil to pay,' Wellington growled, looking between the lieutenant and the corporal. 'Hard marching. Hard fighting. Can I count on you both?'

'Of course, sir,' Fraser said smartly. Plunket just nodded.

'And you, Mister Smith.' Wellington turned his attention back to the smarting spymaster. 'You do your grubby little business well, though I disapprove of much of it. I expect you to continue with your efforts. The French must be harried, sir, *harried!* Never given a moment's peace, whether it's by the partisans, or the men I give you to do your work. Will you make use of these two again?'

He gestured at Fraser and Plunket.

'A young man who speaks good Spanish, and the army's best marksman?' Simpson responded and, to Wellington's surprise, smiled. 'Oh, I believe I can find work for them without end.'

Wellington grunted and looked back at the unlikely pair.

'Well? I won't order you into Simpson's service. You've done enough to warrant never seeing this blasted fellow ever again. But the army relies on the business he and his kind oversees. In the next few months, I suspect that will be truer than ever. What do you say?'

'I'm at your disposal, Your Grace,' Fraser said without any hesitation. Wellington looked at Plunket, holding his pale blue eyes unflinchingly. Eventually, the rifleman gave his own reply.

'If the army wants me to do Simpson's bidding, then I will. I've got to keep being useful.'

'There are worse mottos to live by,' Wellington supposed. 'Very well then. You may have a couple of days here in Lisbon, to see to your own affairs and, God willing, to find some rest. Take Christmas as well. After that, you're to report to Mister Simpson for your next assignment. We've got a war to win. Dismissed.'

Acknowledgements

My thanks to my editor, Amanda, for steering me through this project, and to the wider Rebellion publishing team for making it happen. I hope that fans of the Sniper Elite franchise enjoy this small contribution to a great series.

About the Author

Robbie MacNiven is a Scottish author and historian. His published fiction includes over a dozen novels, many fantasy or sci-fi works for IPs such as Marvel's X-Men and Warhammer 40,000. He has also worked on narrative and character dialogue for multiple digital games (SMITE: Blitz and Age of Sigmar: Storm Ground) and has penned the scripts for two graphic novels and two comics, for Osprey Publishing and Commando Comics respectively. In 2022 his X-Men novel "First Team" won a Scribe Award.

On the non-fiction front, Robbie specialises in Early Modern military history, particularly focusing on the 18th century. He has a PhD in American Revolutionary War massacres from the University of Edinburgh – where he won the Compton Prize for American History – and an MLitt in War Studies from the University of Glasgow.

Outside of work and writing, his passions include re-enacting and gaming. He is thirty-two years old, and prefers cats to dogs (though not by much).

www.ingramcontent.com/pod-product-compliance
Lightning Source LLC
La Vergne TN
LVHW091143080826
845145LV00008B/2240

* 9 7 8 1 8 3 7 8 6 6 5 5 7 *